The Rabbit Ate My Homework

Other books by Rachel Elizabeth Cole

The Rabbit Ate My Flip-Flops
The Rabbit Ate My Hall Pass

Coming Soon

The Rabbit Ate My Snow Pants

Plus more *The Rabbit Ate My ...* books!

The Rabbit Ate My Homework

Rachel Elizabeth Cole

Illustrated by Deanna Dionne

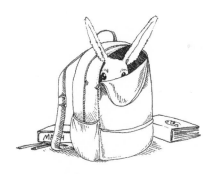

Tangled Oak Press, 2014

ISBN: 9780991766727

Cover by Littera Designs

First Edition

Library and Archives Canada Cataloguing in Publication

Cole, Rachel Elizabeth, 1976-, author
        The rabbit ate my homework / written by Rachel Elizabeth Cole; illustrated by Deanna Dionne.

Issued in print and electronic formats.
ISBN 978-0-9917667-2-7 (pbk.).--ISBN 978-0-9917667-3-4 (ebook)

        I. Dionne, Deanna, illustrator II. Title.

PS8605.O438R32 2014   jC813'.6   C2014-905727-X
                                               C2014-905728-8

To my husband and sons

And, of course, to Gus

Table of Contents

1
The Ride

Most Sundays, I'd rather sleep in. But today when I open my eyes and see the crooked square of sunlight reflecting on the wall over my head, I practically bounce out of bed. For weeks Dad has been promising to take me mountain biking on the trails in the woods behind our house, but every weekend there's been something to stop it from happening. Dad's been too busy. Too tired. Too grumpy. And last week it poured rain all weekend. Always something.

But Friday night, when he got home from work, Dad promised if the weather was good this weekend, we'd go bike riding. Well, taking a look out the window at the bright blue sky, I'd say today is about perfect. The heavy, grey rain clouds have broken up into fluffy cotton puffs and the sun is shining. Actually shining.

1

I dress quickly and race downstairs to grab some breakfast.

"What is that giant burning orb in the sky?" Mom says when I walk into the kitchen. She squints out the window like she's never seen the sun before.

"I don't know." I laugh, even though I've heard the joke too many times. "We better call The Weather Network and ask."

While Mom empties the dishwasher, I grab a bowl and fill it with Cheerios and milk.

I'm just sitting down to eat when Dad walks into the kitchen and beelines for the coffee maker. He's dressed in the holey old shorts and tee shirt he wears to do yard work.

"I thought we were going mountain bike riding," I say, staring at my Cheerios.

"The lawn's not going to cut itself, Drew."

I slump down in my chair.

"Look, we'll go after lunch, okay?"

"Sure." I tap the Cheerios bobbing in my bowl with my spoon.

"I have an idea," Mom says. "Why don't you help your dad? I'm sure there's something you can do. Rake the yard? Pull some weeds? 'Many hands make light work.'"

"It's okay, Jess," Dad says. "I'll take care of it." He slurps his coffee and heads out to the garage.

Mom gives me a reassuring smile. "He shouldn't be too long, Drew. There's still lots of time to go bike riding."

I go into the living room and hunt for the remote control between the couch cushions. I can hear my annoying six-year-old sister, Libby, upstairs singing "Bibbidi Bobbidi Boo" at the top of her lungs. Outside, I hear the lawnmower roar to life. I find the remote and flip on the TV, turning it up loud enough to tune both sounds out.

I'm just getting into the first episode of the SpongeBob Marathon playing on YTV, when the garage door slams and Dad stalks inside.

"Are you done already?" I hop up from the couch.

"No, I am *not* done." Dad grumbles something under his breath and stomps into the kitchen. "Do you know where my Phillips screwdriver is?" he yells back.

"Um, no."

He comes back in the living room. "You sure? You didn't touch it?"

"No, Dad. I promise I haven't."

"Well, I can't find it. If you've walked off with it somewhere, there's going to be trouble."

He stomps back into the garage and the door slams behind him.

I slump back on the couch.

Goodbye bike ride.

Just then Mom comes upstairs from the basement with a basket of laundry.

"Oh," she says when she sees me sitting on the couch. "I thought you two would be gone already."

"I think the lawnmower broke," I say.

Mom's face scrunches into a frown. "I better go see how he's making out. Maybe it's just a quick fix. Do you think you can take this into the kitchen for me?" She holds out the basket.

I take it from her.

"Thanks, Drew." She plants a kiss on the top of my head and ruffles my hair.

I carry the basket into the kitchen. From the window I can see them talking, Dad's head bent over the taken-apart lawnmower, Mom standing with her arms crossed.

The only way I'm going bike riding is if I go by myself. I set the laundry basket on the counter, then go find my bike helmet and shoes and head out to the garage.

I get the key from its hiding place under an old can of paint and unlock my bike.

"Where're you going, Drew?" Libby pops her head out the garage door.

I clip the strap on my bike helmet under my chin. "Where do you think?"

"Dad says you can't go into the woods."

"I know that." I roll my eyes. Ever since Nana and Papa gave me my new bike, Dad's got a million rules about it:

"Lock it up when you're not riding it!"

"No jumps!"

"Don't leave it in the driveway!"

"Quit skidding to a stop!"

You'd think it was his bike, not mine.

"Look, I'm just going to ride up and down the street," I say.

"Can I come too?"

"In that?" Today, she's wearing a shiny pink princess dress that's so long she's bunched up the front into a ball to keep from tripping on it. And the pair of Mom's high heels she's got on her feet aren't about to make walking any easier. Forget bike riding. "Besides, you can't even ride a bike yet."

"I can ride my scooter."

"Barely." I can just see how that would go. Pedal two feet. Stop for Libby to catch up. Pedal another two feet. Stop. Repeat. Might as well not even bother riding my bike. I could push it faster. "Look, I just want to be by myself, okay?"

She sticks her lower lip out at me, but goes back inside, letting the garage door slam behind her.

I better get going before she finds Mom and convinces her that I need to take her with me. I roll my bike down to the curb, stuff my earbuds in my ears, crank up the music on my iPod, and start pedaling.

2
One. Two. Three.

I've ridden up and down the street a dozen times already and I'm bored. I pedal to the end of the street where two big cement barriers sit like guards, protecting the pavement and sidewalks from being taken over by the forest on the other side. A narrow path winds its way between the shaggy cedars and around a corner out of view. I'm tempted to push my bike past the barriers, onto the trail, and start pedaling as fast as I can. I stare down the trail a moment longer, then I turn and start back the way I came.

Mr. Harvey is walking down the sidewalk with his little white fluffball of a dog. Probably just come back from a walk.

"Afternoon," he says, with a nod. At least I think that's what he says. I can't actually hear him over the music playing on my iPod.

I nod back and keep pedaling.

About halfway up the block, I pass my best friend Quentin's old house. Last summer his family moved all the way into town and now a family with two little girls lives there. There's no one outside right now, but pink girl toys are scattered all over the front lawn. I wish Quentin was here now. Maybe Dad would let us go riding up in the woods together.

In no time, I'm at the other end of the street where it joins Arbutus Ridge Road. I think about stopping and turning back again, but one more time up and down the street and I'm going to go crazy. I'll just ride up to the next street where the new houses are being built, and then I'll turn around and coast down the hill back home. It won't take too long.

I round the corner and pedal past the school bus stop. The road is getting steeper, so I gear down and stand on my pedals. The sun has climbed higher in the sky and is beaming down on my back and neck and I'm starting to get really hot. This road doesn't seem so steep when you're walking or riding in a car, but on a bike it's a whole other story. I stop for a breather and realize I'm right across the road from the trail where Dad and I would've gone riding together. The narrow dirt path angles off into the woods and disappears behind the trees. It looks a lot flatter and shadier than the road.

For a few seconds, I lean on my bike deciding what to do. I know I should probably head back home. Maybe Dad is done with the mower and will want to go for a bike ride after all. I think about the lawnmower parts scattered all over the backyard. Probably not. With my luck, he'll be working on that mower until it's dark.

I get off my bike, check for cars, and walk across the street. I push my bike through the shallow ditch, climb back on and start riding down the trail. It is definitely cooler in the trees and I find myself pedaling faster to stay warm.

Not far along the trail there's a huge cedar stump from when they first logged the mountainside, back when the trees grew so big it took ten people to link hands around the trunks. There's a couple other stumps like this around, but none of them are quite as big. The middle is hollowed out and when Quentin and I were little kids, we used to climb inside and pretend it was a fort, or a pirate ship, or the Millennium Falcon.

I keep pedaling. Around another corner, over a small hill, and down the other side. My bike eats up the trail like it's hungry for more. The trail starts to go downhill and I speed up. Around another corner and another. My bike is whizzing along and I'm barely touching the pedals. It feels awesome. Then I spot the jump. A giant cedar root banked with dirt creates the perfect natural jump. I can't resist. I turn my bike in that direction.

One.

Two.

Three.

I hit the jump and a giant burst of adrenaline shoots through my veins. For a second, it feels like I'm flying as I soar over the jump. Then I land with a sickening *CRACK!* and the front end of the bike folds underneath me. I fly over the handlebars and watch in heart-thumping dread as the ground comes up at me in slow motion. And then *THWUMP!* I collide with the ground and all the air is knocked out of my lungs.

For a long moment I lie there on the ground, not able to breathe, not able to move. Finally, I can roll into a sitting position and brush the pine needles and dirt off me. I pull my earbuds from my ears and glance around. A bird flaps overhead and somewhere a woodpecker is drilling a hole in a tree, but otherwise the woods are dead quiet. My shoulder aches where I landed on it, but I can move it so it doesn't seem to be broken. My bike, on the other hand, is lying in a twisted heap beside me. My brand new bike.

I feel sick to my stomach. Dad is going to kill me.

Stiffly, I get to my feet. The knees of my jeans are caked in dirt. I do my best to brush them off, then check my bike over. The suspension fork that holds the front wheel in place is broken. When I lift it up, the wheel wobbles like a loose tooth. How am I even going to get it home like this? I glance up the steep hill and my stomach sinks. Nothing to do but start pushing.

It seems to take forever to push my bike back up the trail to where it levels off again. At this rate it's going to be dark by the time I get home. I am so dead. No, I'm beyond dead.

How am I even going to explain to Mom and Dad what happened? I run a bunch of explanations through my head.

"It was a pothole. A big one!"

"Maybe it was broken when we got it."

"Broken? What? Where?"

"Libby did it!"

I round another bend and the huge tree stump comes into view. I get an idea. What if I hide my bike in there? Just until I can figure out what to do. I'm sure with Quentin's help I can figure out a plan to fix it so Mom and Dad will never know better.

I push my bike through the big gap in the side of the stump, lay it on its side, and bury it in leaves. I'm not too worried about anyone finding it. None of the kids come into the woods anymore. Not since some homeless guys have been spotted camped out further up the trail and all the parents freaked out and made a No Woods rule. Only the high schoolers sometimes come up here to party. And not that often because the police usually show up and chase them all out.

Satisfied with my plan, I squeeze out of the stump and head back to the trail.

Libby is waiting for me. Her arms are crossed and her lower lip is sticking out. Again. At least she's changed out of that stupid dress.

"You're not supposed to be in the woods!" she says. "I'm telling!" She spins on her heel and starts marching back down the trail.

My heartbeat speeds up. If she tells I am in so much trouble.

"You can't tell!" I yell after her. "Then you'll have to tell Mom and Dad you were in the woods. You'll get in trouble, too!"

That stops her. She turns and frowns at me. "Where's your bike?"

I think fast. "Just up the trail. The, um, chain fell off. I need to go get some grease." I study her face close-ly. Does she know something?

"What happened to your jeans?" Libby points at the dirt stains on my knees.

"I, uh, fell off my bike when the chain came off." She's asking an awful lot of questions. I need to distract her. "Look, you better get home before Mom and Dad start to wonder where you are." I try to guide her back down the trail, but she pushes my hand away.

"Why didn't you wait for me?" she says.

"I thought you were going to play with your dolls."

"No, I said I wanted to come, too. I went to ask Mom."

"Sorry, I didn't know." I shrug. "Maybe next time. Come on. Let's head home. I need to get that grease."

I start walking and glance back to be sure she's following. She's still standing on the trail staring at the huge stump.

"Y'know, there's bears up here," I say.

That gets her going. She trots down the trail after me and doesn't slow down until we're safely back on the road.

As soon as we're home, I go into the garage and make a bunch of noise hunting for the grease until I hear the front door slam and I'm sure Libby has gone into the house. Then I run back up the street and around the corner. I plop down under a tree and count to 100. While I'm counting, I study the tube of grease in my hand. I sure wish this was all my bike needed. I'm pretty sure it's going to need a whole new front suspension fork. How much is that going to cost? And how am I even going to get it? I lose count somewhere around 69 or 70, so I start over. When I lose count again, I decide I've probably been gone long enough. I sneak back home through the neighbour's yard and come in through the back gate, hoping Libby isn't watching out the front window for me.

Dad is still in the backyard with his tools. But the

lawnmower is now looking more like it's supposed to and less like a bunch of used parts. He spots me and waves me over. "Look, Drew, I know you're disappointed we didn't get to do that bike ride today. But we've all got responsibilities and we have to take care of those first. Maybe next weekend, okay?"

"Uh, sure," I manage to mumble. I'm not sure what else to say. All I know is there's not gonna be a next weekend if I can't figure out a way to fix my bike.

3
The Box

The next day at school, I can barely concentrate. All I can think about is my bike. What if I can't fix it? What if somebody finds it? What if Dad notices it's gone?

What if? What if? What if?

I chew the end of my pencil. After dinner last night, I'd snuck back up to the woods before it got dark to check on my bike. I was getting worried someone might find it and steal it. But it was exactly where I left it buried in leaves, safe inside the big old stump.

Still, I know it's only a matter of time before Dad notices it's gone. I need to make a plan. I need to do something.

As soon as the bell rings for lunch, Quentin and I head outside to the corner of the playing field where the trees overhang the grass. This part of the field is always wet and walking on it is more like walking on a soggy sponge than grass, but it's our corner and nobody ever bugs us here. Even though it hasn't rained since Saturday, the whole place is flooded with puddles. Three big rocks are sticking out of the puddles like islands in the ocean. We jump the puddles and climb up on them. While Quentin chows down on his tuna sandwich, I tell him about my bike.

"Dude, you need to 'fess up," Quentin says. He points at my chocolate chip granola bar in my lunch kit. "You gonna eat that?"

I hand it over. I'm not even a little bit hungry. "'Fess up? My dad will kill me!"

"It's not going to get any better, the longer you wait." He unwraps the granola bar and stuffs it into his mouth whole. The kid is part sea gull. I've never seen him choke.

"Easy for you to say. Your dad's so laid back."

"You haven't seen him when he's really mad," he says around the mouthful of granola bar. He chews a little longer and swallows. "Look, if you're worried about your dad freaking out, tell your mom."

He has a point. Mom wouldn't blow her top like Dad would. But then she'd tell Dad and then he'd blow his top. I can't see how telling her is going to work any better than telling him in the first place.

"Can't you just help me fix it?"

Quentin sighs. "Sorry, dude. I got nothin'."

🥕 🥕 🥕

Finally school ends and Libby and I catch the bus home. It pulls up at the top of our road and the driver opens the door. I grab my backpack, and follow Libby off the bus. As we trudge home, I pull out my iPod and check the time. 3:36. I've got less than an hour and a half to get my bike fixed before Mom and Dad get home from work. But I've got a plan. All I need is the number to the bike shop in town. I only hope I've got enough money in my piggybank to pay for the repairs.

I'm putting my iPod back in my pocket when Libby grabs my arm and just about knocks it right out of my hand. "Would you watch it?" I snap.

"Drew, what is that?"

"What is what?"

"*That!*"

I glance up. There's a small, battered cardboard box sitting in the ditch on the side of the road, about ten feet ahead of us. "It's a box. In the ditch."

"No, can't you hear that sound?"

"What sound?"

"That sound!"

I pull out my earbuds. At first all I can hear is a

squirrel chattering in the woods beside us and a car roaring by on Arbutus Ridge Road behind us. Then I hear it: There's a sort of a scrabbling, scratching sound coming from inside the box, interrupted now and again by a loud *THUMP!*

"I'm scared." Libby clutches my arm.

"Oh, Libby. Don't be such a baby. It's probably just a rat." Mom and Dad are always complaining about the rats getting into our garbage. Last summer Dad even found a giant rats' nest in his tool shed. He had to call the exterminator to get rid of them. "Come on." I peel Libby's fingers from my arm and start walking again.

She doesn't budge.

"Come on," I say.

"I don't like rats." She shivers. "Their tails are creepy."

"Libby, *come on*." I grab for her arm.

"No!" She swats my hand away. "You have to chase it away. I won't move until it's gone. Make it go away, Drew."

"It's just a stupid rat."

Libby crosses her arms.

It's pretty clear Libby isn't going anywhere until the big scary rat inside the box is gone. I throw my hands up. "Fine!"

Grabbing a stick from the side of the road, I eye the box. It's just a plain old brown cardboard box, the flaps folded closed on the top. The scrabbling sound has stopped. Maybe Libby's shrieking has scared whatever it is away. I take a few steps towards it. Then another. And another. Just as I'm reaching out with the stick to pry open one of the flaps . . . *THUMP!*

I yelp and jump back.

Libby giggles.

"Shut up!" I snap. "Chicken."

Libby sticks out her tongue at me. "You're the chicken."

THUMP! THUMP!

Whatever's inside is much bigger than a rat. My stomach tightens. Now I'm not sure I want to see what's in the box. I glance at Libby. She'll never let me live it down if I wuss out now. I take a deep breath. Then I tear the flaps open, kick the box over, and jump back—far enough back, I hope, to be out of the reach of Godzilla-sized rat teeth.

Libby gasps. "A bunny!"

"A what?"

Crouching on the ground next to the overturned box is a small, caramel-coloured rabbit with huge ears.

"Aw! Look at him. He's so cute." Before I can stop her, Libby has scrambled down into the ditch to pet the bunny. "Are you lost, little bunny? Where's your home?" Libby gazes up at me with the same look she gives Mom right before she asks for cookies and ice cream. "He's so cute. Can we take him home?"

"No, we can't. He doesn't belong to us."

"Please! Please! *Please!*"

"No! No! *NO!*"

"But we can't leave him here. What if something bad happens to him?"

"Nothing bad is going to happen to him. Put him back in the box before he runs away." I glance up and down the road, at the houses and driveways on one side, the woods on the other, but there's no one around but me and Libby. People sometimes leave unwanted pets up here. Last year there were a couple cats, a box of kittens, and even a chicken. But whoever left him here is long gone.

"He doesn't want to go back in the box." Libby's bottom lip is stuck out so far it looks like a helicopter could land on it.

"Yes, he *does*." I scoop up the rabbit and put it back into the box. "Look, we can't keep him. You know how

Mom and Dad feel about pets."

Mom and Dad have made it very clear how they feel about pets. They have every reason why we can't have one:

"Mom has allergies."

"We don't have time."

"What if we go on vacation?"

"Pets cost money."

"Who will clean up after it?"

To be honest, I've always wanted a pet—I'd probably go crazy if Dad said we could get a dog—but I've *never* wanted a rabbit. All they do is sit in their cages, eat carrots, and poop. Every summer at the Agri-Fair, they have a rabbit show. Rows and rows of rabbits in cages, sitting there, doing nothing. They're probably the most boring animal alive. "I'm sure someone else will find him," I say. "Come on. We have to get home."

The whole way home, Libby drags her heels, stopping constantly to look back at the box. Finally, I get annoyed with her dawdling and march on ahead. I'm in the house, just hanging up the phone from letting Mom know we're home safe and sound, when Libby wanders into the backyard. Followed closely by one small, caramel-coloured rabbit with huge ears.

"Libby!"

Libby gives me her best innocent look. "I didn't do anything. He followed me home."

The rabbit spots Mom's rose bush, hops over to it, and begins helping itself to the leaves.

"You know when Mom and Dad are at work, I'm the boss. So take that rabbit back to its box and leave it there."

"I tried. He wouldn't stay in the box."

I'll believe that when little sisters stop being such a major pain in the rear end. "Look, we *can't* keep him. I'm going to call the animal shelter. They'll take care of him."

"You can't do that!" Libby's chin wobbles. "They might put him to sleep."

"What? That cute little bunny?" I point at the rabbit. It stops nibbling the rose bush and sits up on its back legs, wiggling its nose. "Are you kidding? I bet they find him a new home tomorrow." I turn to go back inside and find the phone book.

"Andrew Wayne Montgomery," Libby calls from behind me, using her best Mom voice, "if you call, I'll tell Mom and Dad about your bike."

A lead weight drops in my stomach. I cast a sideways glance at Libby. "Oh? What happened to my bike?"

She crosses her arms. "I know where it is. I know you broke it."

I clear my throat. "I don't know what you're talking about."

"I'm not dumb, Drew. You broke it. I saw you."

"No, you didn't!"

"Yes, I did! I followed you after dinner. It's under a bunch of leaves in the big stump. The front wheel is all wobbly."

I shut my mouth. She has me. Guilty as charged. There's no wiggling out of it. "Okay, fine. We can keep him." I grit my teeth as I say it. I can hardly believe I'm agreeing to this. "But it has to be a secret. If anybody finds out we are both in major trouble."

Libby grins at me like she's just won a prize at the fair.

4

Rabbit in the House

Libby, of course, wants to keep the rabbit in her room. "He can sleep in my bed."

"That is the dumbest thing I've ever heard. Why would a rabbit sleep in your bed?"

"Because it's comfy."

Why was I ever dumb enough to think a nosy six-year-old would stay home and mind her own business? "I think he should stay in Dad's tool shed."

"He can't stay there. He'll get cold and lonely and scared."

"Libby, you can't keep him in your room." I can just see how that would go: Mom and Dad would find the rabbit in two seconds flat. Then the questions would start:

"How did this rabbit get here?"

"Who said you could keep a rabbit?"

And Libby would blab everything:

"Drew and I found him in a box on the road."

"Drew said we could keep him."

Yeah, no. I don't think so.

"We have to put him somewhere Mom and Dad will never think to look." I snap my fingers. "I know. We'll put him in the basement."

"Not the basement!"

"Well, where would you put him? *Besides* your bedroom?"

"What about your room?"

"My room?"

"Yeah, Mom and Dad never go in your room."

"No way! There's no way that rabbit is staying in my room."

Libby rolls her eyes. "Why not?"

She has a point. Since I've turned eleven, it seems like Mom and Dad have both gone out of their way to stay out of my room. "Okay, I have an idea. We'll put him in my closet."

"But he'll get scared in there."

"Libby, if you want to keep the rabbit in the house, he has to stay in the closet. Otherwise, Mom and Dad might find him. And we really don't want Mom and Dad to find him. Get it?"

Libby's lower lip juts out again, but she doesn't argue with me anymore.

"Come on." I sigh.

Cleaning out my closet turns out to be a bigger challenge than I expected. I can't even remember the last time I cleaned it, that's how long it's been. There aren't any clothes in there—unless you count the size 6X tuxedo from Uncle Shawn and Aunt Sophie's wedding that's hanging in the back corner—but it's packed with all the old toys and books and stuff I don't play with anymore.

"Why do you have so much junk?" Libby asks, her eyes goggling at the heaping pile about to avalanche down on us.

"It's not *junk*. It's just stuff Mom hasn't taken to the thrift store."

Libby picks out a linty granola bar wrapper, a shoelace, and a Hot Wheels car with no wheels. "Like this stuff?"

I sigh. "Go grab some garbage bags."

Once we've cleared all the stuff out of my closet, we line the carpet with newspaper. Libby gets a doll's bed with a pink blanket—hearts and flowers and all—from her room for the rabbit to sleep on, though I really don't think he needs it. This is a rabbit! But she keeps bringing up my broken bike, so I let her have her way. We also put in a bowl filled with water and a plate with some lettuce and carrots. Besides carrots, I'm not totally sure what rabbits eat, but I remember Nana and Papa complaining about them getting into their vegetable garden last summer, so I figure lettuce is a pretty safe bet.

Then we go back out to the yard to figure out how to get the rabbit into the house. Though I'd been secretly hoping it might have hopped off to join its long-lost wild family in the woods, it's still there nibbling dandelion leaves. It pricks its ears at me as I march over, then it ducks behind the rose bush.

"Here, bunny," I say, snapping my fingers. "Come here, bunny."

From under the bush, the rabbit pokes its nose out and wiggles it at me.

"Come on, bunny." I move towards the rabbit. It hops back behind the bush. I pluck a rose leaf and hold it out to the rabbit. It takes a step forward, its ears pricked, nose wiggling with interest.

"You know you want it. Come and get it."

The rabbit stretches as far as it can to reach the leaf.

"Come on. Just a little closer."

The rabbit inches closer. I hold my breath. It's so close I can almost grab it.

I pounce. The rabbit takes off like a shot. I come up with grass-stained knees and dirt under my fingernails. I thump the ground with my fist. "Just great!"

The rabbit is now perched on the back step, giving Libby and me the same displeased look Mrs. DiCastillo gives us when she catches us running in the halls.

"Aw! Is Drew scaring you?" Libby reaches towards the rabbit, but it flips its ears and hops a few feet away from her. With every step she takes, he hops a few more feet away from her.

"Move over by the gate." I motion to Libby.

She does and the rabbit stops to watch her.

Perfect!

"Come here, already!" I lunge towards the rabbit.

The rabbit runs. I chase. For what seems like forever, we run in figure eights around the backyard, the rabbit dodging and doubling back, hopping through Mom's flowerbeds and around the tool shed, but always staying just out of my reach.

Out of breath, I flop down on the grass. "Okay, rabbit, you win."

The rabbit hops out from behind the rose bush, where it's hidden itself again, wiggles its nose at me, and starts munching grass. A long blade disappears into its mouth like it's on a conveyor belt.

"Wait! I have an idea," Libby says and begins plucking dandelion leaves from the lawn.

The rabbit stops munching to watch her.

She begins laying them in a trail leading into the house.

Soon enough, the bunny is nibbling his way up the steps, onto the porch, through the door, and into the back hall. I hate to admit it, but her plan is bordering on brilliant. Of course, I would rather eat worms than tell her that.

Another trail of dandelion leaves gets the rabbit upstairs and into my room. It sniffs around the door to the closet, like it isn't sure it wants to go inside, but then it spots the carrots and lettuce, and it hops right on in and gets busy munching. When the salad is gone, he sits on his back legs and begins washing his face with his paws.

"Aw! Isn't he so cute?" Libby cries.

"Sure, whatever."

The rabbit licks himself all over, and then he plops down and kicks his back legs out beside him. Libby reaches over and rubs his forehead. The bunny lowers his head to the floor and closes his eyes. "What should we name him?" she says.

"How about Stew?"

"You can't name the bunny Stew!"

"Okay, then: Stupid."

"Drew!" Libby scowls at me. "I think we should call him Precious."

"*Precious*?" I just about gag on the word. "That's a girl's name."

"Maybe the bunny is a girl."

"No way! This is definitely a boy bunny."

Libby crosses her arms. "How would you know the difference?"

Well, she's right. I don't know the difference. But there's no way we are calling this rabbit Precious. "Because he's got big ears," I say. "Boy bunnies always have bigger ears than girl bunnies. Don't you know anything?"

Libby doesn't reply. She sits there, stroking the rabbit. He's flattened himself onto the floor, loving the attention. "He's so little. I think we should call him Tiny."

"Tiny is a dumb name."

"No, *Stew* is a dumb name!" Libby stabs me with a glare. "You like Tiny, don't you, little bunny?"

"You know what? Name him Twinkle Toes Bubble Bunny for all I care."

Why, oh why did I have to break my bike?

Once "Tiny" is comfortable in his new home, I tell Libby we should get started on our homework—her in her room and me in mine—so Mom and Dad won't wonder what we've been doing all afternoon. Really, I just want a minute to myself to call the bike shop. Libby, of course, can't focus on anything but the rabbit. Every time I turn around she's sneaking back into my room to pet it or play with it.

The rest of the afternoon basically goes like this:

Libby (squealing): "Aw! Drew, look! He can wiggle his tail!"

Me: "Great, Libby. Would you close the closet door before he gets out?"

Libby (squealing again): "Drew, come see! He's washing his ears! Aw! What a cute little bunny!"

Me: "Yeah, very cute, Libby. Now please leave him *alone*!"

Libby (squealing yet again): "Drew! Do something! He pooped on his bed!"

Me: "That's what bunnies do. Now would you go do your homework?"

Libby (squealing even more): "Drew! Drew! He got out! What do I do?"

Me: "*Libby!*"

After a whole bunch more running and chasing and even more squealing, I manage to get the rabbit back into the closet and Libby sitting at her white princess desk with her spelling homework—just in time for Mom and Dad to get home from work.

"Do not say a word about the rabbit. Got it?"

Libby nods.

"I mean it. Not *one* word. Or we're both in *big* trouble."

"Okay, I promise." Libby crosses her heart and rolls her eyes.

5

So Dead

Hi, I'm calling about getting a bike fixed?" I'm in the bathroom with the water running and the fan on so Libby won't overhear me. Unfortunately, neither can the guy on the phone.

"Sorry, what was that?" he says.

I turn off the tap. "I need to get my bike fixed."

"Oh, sure thing. What's the problem?"

"Um, the front fork is broken."

"Suspension fork?"

"Yeah."

"You're probably looking at seventy-five to one hundred dollars to replace it."

"How much?" I choke. I don't have that kind of money. I'd emptied out every last penny from my piggybank and I only had $39.12. I thought about borrowing the rest from Libby but when I checked her piggybank, she only had $6.76. Not nearly enough.

"It might not need replacing. Can you bring the bike in to take a look at it?"

"Um, not really. You can't come pick it up?"

The guy laughs. "Sorry, kid. It doesn't work that way. You have to bring it in."

"Okay, I'll, uh, thanks."

"No problem."

I hang up the phone and sink down on the edge of the tub. Now what am I going to do?

"Drew, are you done?" Libby bangs on the bathroom door. "I gotta go!"

I leave the bathroom to my little sister and head for my room.

A new Skype message chirps on my computer. It's Quentin.

Qchow99: Hey

Me: Yeah

Qchow99: Sup?

Me: I'm so dead

Qchow99: ?

Me: I can't fix my bike

Qchow99: Yeah ur dead

Me: Not funny

Qchow99: Sorry

Me: You got $50 I can borrow?

Qchow99: No

Me: ☹

Qchow99: So what r u gonna do?

Me: I dunno

Qchow99: Get a job?

Me: No time.

Qchow99: Dude ur so dead

Me: Not HELPING

Qchow99: Sorry

Me: Can you ask your brother?

Qchow99: I can't I owe him $20

Me: What about your sister?

Qchow99: I owe her $10

Me: Is there anyone you DON'T owe money to?

Qchow99: U

Me: I'm so dead.

Qchow99: Blame it on Libby

Me: She can't even ride a bike!

Qchow99: Then I dunno

Me: Me either

Qchow99: Gtg

Me: Ok

Qchow99: Cya

I close the chat box and stare at the screen. Maybe Quentin's right. Maybe I can get a job. Matt Tremont told me last summer he made a pile of money mowing people's lawns. He made almost $60 in one weekend.

I glance out the window. It's raining pretty hard now. I don't think I'll be mowing any lawns today.

If it was winter and it snowed, I could make money shovelling driveways. Fall, and I could rake leaves. But what could I do in the pouring rain in April? Carry people's umbrellas?

Downstairs, the door to the garage slams. Hard.

"Drew? Drew, where are you?!" It's Dad. And he sounds mad. Real mad.

A bunch of different thoughts cram into my head at once. The first is: *He's found my bike.* The second is: *He knows about the rabbit.* And the last is: *I need more than $50 to save me now.*

"*Drew?!*" Dad's voice is louder and—if it's even possible—madder.

I swallow. Guess there's no avoiding it. I log off the Internet and push my chair back from my desk.

"Oh, Drew!" Libby bounces into the room wearing bunny ears and one of her white princess dresses with what looks like fifty cotton balls taped to the butt. Crooked whiskers are drawn in black felt pen on her face. She stops, tries to wiggle her nose at me, and says, "Who do I look like?"

"Gee, I dunno. My annoying little sister in a stupid rabbit costume?"

"I'm Tiny, you dummy! You're never any fun!" Libby sticks her tongue out at me. "By the way, Dad's calling you!"

"Duh! I know that." I glare at her. "Now get out of my room."

"There's no carrots in here anyway," she says and hops out.

"*DREW!*"

"Coming!" I take a quick peek in my closet. The rabbit's curled up in the corner of the closet like a fuzzy bunny slipper. He looks asleep, but his eyes are wide open. Either way, he doesn't look like he's about to escape or be discovered. I close the door and head downstairs to face my judge, jury, and executioner.

Dad's waiting for me by the door to the garage, his arms crossed, his face dark red. Dad has red hair, so he goes red in the face easy, but this was the reddest I've ever seen. It's the same red colour cartoon characters' heads go just before they explode. "How many times do I have to call you?"

"Sorry, I, uh—"

"Where is your bike?"

"I, um—"

"How many times have I told you that you have to put it away, Drew?"

"I, uh—"

"Did you put your bike away or not?"

"No, I—"

"Well, it's gone. Do you understand that? Stolen! Didn't I tell you this would happen?"

"But, uh—"

"I'm calling the police."

I'm so dead.

🥕　　🥕　　🥕

The whole time Dad's dialling the phone—somehow he manages to turn something that should take five seconds into fifteen minutes—he's nonstop lecturing me about my bike. How I should've been more responsible. How I could've shown Nana and Papa more appreciation by taking better care of it. As if I don't know all this. As if I don't feel bad enough already.

"Have you got anything to say for yourself?" he asks.

I swallow. Well, of course I do. But where do I start? I can't exactly say, "Well, Dad, my bike isn't actually stolen. Remember how you said no jumps? Yeah, well, I went off a jump in the woods and I broke my bike. Then I hid it under an old stump until I could figure out what to do with it." Somehow I can see his head really exploding if I say that. I swallow again. Right at this moment, I wish I had a dad like Quentin's. He seems to find something funny in everything. You could tell him the world's going to be hit by a giant comet tomorrow and all life is going to be wiped out and he'd make a joke about it. My dad? He'd probably find a way to make it my fault.

But before I can say anything, Dad turns and starts talking into the phone. "Yes, hello. I'd like to report a stolen bike."

Too late.

I listen with a growing sense of dread as he describes my bike to the officer. This is bad. No, this is worse than bad. Lying to the police is a crime, isn't it? I need to tell him the truth.

"Uh, Dad," I say, but he's not listening. He's pacing up and down the living room floor, like the tiger we saw at the Greater Vancouver Zoo last year.

"It's a five-hundred-dollar bicycle. Only three months old."

"Dad?"

He waves me away. "The serial number?" he says, then clears his throat. "Er, I'm afraid we don't have it. The bike was a gift from my parents. . . . Y'know, they might have it. I'll ask them."

He covers the receiver and turns to me. "The police officer wants to know when you think your bike was stolen."

"I, uh . . ." I don't know what to say. I don't want to lie. But Dad is standing there staring at me in that way that says if I don't come up with an answer pretty quick, his fuse is going to blow. "I don't know?"

Dad scowls. "Well, when were you last riding it?"

"Um, oh yeah. Yesterday afternoon." At least that's the truth.

"And where was that?"

I swallow. I can't exactly tell him the truth about that. Or can I? "I was riding it on the street for a bit." That's mostly the truth. I rode it up the street to the woods.

"You left it on the *street*?"

Wrong answer.

"What? No!" I say quickly. "I, uh—"

"Well, did you lock it up like you're supposed to or not?"

"Um, no."

Dad sighs. "Then where did you leave it?"

I gaze down at the table top. There are a few small rings of dried milk that hadn't been wiped up after breakfast. "The yard, I guess?"

"He says he left it in the yard. We *usually* keep the bikes locked in the garage," Dad says, giving me a hard stare.

I am so dead. No, I'm deader than dead. Might as well go buy myself a coffin now.

"Yes, yes. All right. Thanks very much for your time." Dad hangs up the phone and lets out a loud sigh. Then he turns to me. He crosses his arms and leans back a bit so he's looking at me straight down his nose. "Drew, do you know what probation is?"

"No, not really."

"Well, you're going to find out. I could ground you.

I *should* ground you. But I'm letting you off the hook. Mess up again even one more time, though, and you're grounded—till you graduate high school. Get it?"

I try to swallow, but the muscles in my throat have tied themselves into a giant knot. I try to answer, but the giant knot keeps the words from coming out. So I just nod.

"All right, go finish your homework or whatever it was you were doing."

I nod again and shuffle off to the stairs.

"You better hope the police find your bike, Drew," Dad says after me.

Libby pops her head out of the kitchen as I pass. I can tell by the smug look on her face she's heard everything. She looks so pleased with herself her head looks like it could swell up and float away like a balloon.

"Sorry about your bike getting stolen, Drew," she says and then winks at me. Or at least she tries to wink. It looks more like she's got something caught in her eye.

I groan. I hope the police never find my bike. I don't want it found. Ever.

6
"Good night, Rabbit."

Dinner is awfully quiet. Normally, Mom and Dad talk about work. What jobs they're doing. What people at work are driving them crazy. How they both need a raise. Or a vacation. Or both.

Stuff like that.

Dad works for a property development company. He likes to tell Mom all about the big jobs they're doing. Right now they're building a bunch of big expensive houses on the golf course. Dad thinks it'll help the economy. Mom thinks it'll make more traffic and more accidents.

Mom works for an insurance company and knows lots of statistics about car accidents and unsafe driving and stuff. Which means I probably won't be allowed to get my driver's license until I'm twenty-one.

Tonight, Dad's probably thinking of every little thing I can possibly do that he could ground me for. Mom's probably thinking how Dad needs to lighten up sometimes. And I'm thinking how dead I'm going to be if Mom and Dad find out about the stupid rabbit. Or my bike. Or both.

"So what did you do at school today?" Dad asks me.

I shrug. "Not much."

Libby pipes up, "Mom, did you know bunnies like to eat dandelions? They—ouch! Drew! What'd you kick me for?"

"Drew!" Mom says.

"Sorry, it was an accident," I say, glaring at Libby.

"Keep your feet under your chair, Drew." Mom gives me a tired look. "What were you saying, sweetie?" She turns back to Libby.

Libby glances at me. "Just something I, um, learned today."

"Libby was reading a library book about rabbits," I say.

"Oh, that's nice. Maybe we can read it together at bedtime."

Libby looks panicked. "I, um, don't have it," she stammers. "I, um, lost it."

"What? Where?" Mom says, alarmed.

"Don't you mean you left it at school?" I say.

"Oh, yeah. That's right. I, um, forgot it." Libby fiddles with her fork.

Mom gives us both a confused look.

"You know," says Dad. "My sister had a rabbit when we were kids."

"Really?" Libby says, brightening.

"Yeah, it died."

I can't help it. I laugh.

"Drew!" Libby says. "That's not nice. Poor little bunny."

"Oh, it wasn't poor or little." Dad leans on the table. "It was this huge white thing. Ate everything in sight. And it would bite. One time it nearly took my finger off. I still have the scar." He holds out his hand to show us the faded white scar tissue on his knuckle.

"Ouch," I say.

Libby looks horrified.

"Yeah, that rabbit was mean through and through," Dad says. "Her name was Mrs. B. and the 'B' didn't stand for Bunny."

"Todd!" Mom glares at Dad.

"What?" Dad says. "I'm just telling them the truth."

"Well, when I was a little girl, my best friend, Natalie, had a bunny. He had floppy ears and a spot on his nose that looked like a moustache. I thought he was the cutest little thing," Mom says, picking up the salad bowl. "Would anyone like more salad?"

"I would, please." Libby holds out her plate.

"Are you sure? You don't usually like salad."

"Oh, I'm super hungry tonight, Mom."

"I can tell," Mom says, scooping lettuce onto Libby's empty plate.

After dinner, Mom goes into the kitchen to clean up and Dad takes his laptop and heads to the couch to watch the hockey game.

Libby and I clear the table. As soon as we're done, she wants to go check on the rabbit. I don't want to make Mom and Dad suspicious, but there's no way I'm letting Libby into my room by herself. So we sneak upstairs.

The rabbit doesn't seem to have moved an inch from the spot in the corner. Except he seems to have decided the doll's bed makes a good bathroom, because there's a yellowish-orange puddle on it and a growing mound of poops.

"Gross!" I plug my nose.

Libby kneels in the closet doorway and strokes the rabbit's nose. "Naughty rabbit. You made your new bed all dirty."

"And you wanted him to sleep in your bed?" I pretend to barf.

The rabbit yawns and stretches, giving his ears a good shake, and then he hops over to nudge Libby's knee.

"Are you hungry?" she asks as she empties her pockets of salad, green beans, potatoes, and bread crusts.

"Libby! That was supposed to be your dinner."

"Well, he needs to eat too."

The rabbit mows through the salad and the bread crusts in no time, but he turns up his nose at the cooked veggies.

"I guess he doesn't like potatoes and green beans." Libby shrugs.

"Guess not."

Just then, Mom calls Libby to take her bath and get ready for bed.

"You better go. You don't want her to come looking for you." I nod towards the rabbit.

Libby looks disappointed, but she leaves the room, shutting the door behind her. If only it was this easy to get rid of her *every* day.

The minute she's out of my room, I boot up my computer and check to see if Quentin is online. He's not. Darn. I could really use some help with this whole rabbit situation. I just know Libby's gonna give everything away before long and then I'm the one who's gonna end up grounded for life. I really need a Plan B. And fast.

Why did I have to break my bike? Even if I managed to get the money somewhere to fix it and got it to the shop to be fixed, it's not like I could ever ride it. What could I say? "Oh, look, Dad. I found my bike! Guess it

45

was lost, not stolen!" Yeah, no. I don't think so.

"No thanks to you!" I glare at the rabbit. He's busy grooming himself on the floor of the closet and doesn't seem the least bit interested in what I'm doing.

Angrily, I grab a piece of paper off my desk, crumple it into tight ball and chuck it at the rabbit. It bounces off the wall above his head and lands on the floor in front of him. His ears shoot straight up and he jumps back, his nose going a mile a minute. Then he stretches his head out and sniffs the paper cautiously. When it doesn't move, he nudges it with his nose. Then he starts nibbling a corner.

I laugh, because it's funny. Then I feel bad. "Sorry," I say. "I've had a bit of a bad day."

The rabbit doesn't respond. He just keeps nibbling the paper, one long ear pointed in my direction like an antenna.

My brain hurts and I don't want to think about rabbits or bikes or blackmail anymore. I decide to play my favourite online game, Alien Doom, to take my mind off the mess I'm in. I've been playing Alien Doom for weeks and I haven't got past Level 10 yet. Maybe tonight will be the night.

The first Alien appears on the screen, and I blast it. Then the next. In no time, I'm totally focused on the game. I easily finish off the first eight levels, but Level 9 is more of a challenge. It takes some fast thinking and quick reflexes to navigate the asteroid field and destroy all the alien ships. I'm about to blast the last ship and move on to Level 10, when I hear a weird thump from under the desk. Something furry nudges my foot. What? I glance down. The rabbit is under the desk, sniffing at the computer cords hanging there. Before I can do anything, it takes a huge chomp out of one of them.

"Hey! Whoa! What are you doing?" I grab for the rabbit, but he scoots out from underneath and runs back into the closet. He sits there, glaring at me. And there's no mistaking it. This rabbit was glaring at me.

"Bad rabbit!" I say, and bend down to check out the damage. He's nipped the plastic coating right off the cord, exposing the copper wire underneath. "Bad rabbit!"

He doesn't seem to care. He's turned his back to me and is nibbling the newspaper again.

I look up at the computer screen. A big orange GAME OVER is flashing at me. Stupid rabbit. I was so close!

With a sigh, I lean back in my chair. Maybe video games aren't the greatest idea right now. Not with a cord-chomping rabbit on the loose. I shut down the computer and wedge my chair under the desk so the rabbit hopefully won't get in there again.

Grabbing the latest issue of *Galactic Bounty Hunter*, I stretch out on my bed to read. But I can't focus on the comic book. All I can think about is the stupid rabbit. I knew there was a reason I never wanted a rabbit. The thing just attempted computicide.

The door to my room creaks open, making me jump. But it's only Libby.

"Would you knock?" I scowl at her over the top of my comic book. "You freaked me right out. I thought maybe you were Mom."

"I want to say good night to Tiny."

"Make it quick," I say. "But don't think just because the rabbit's in here, you can come into my room whenever you want."

Libby gets down on her knees and gives the rabbit a hug and a kiss. Suddenly she squeals. "He licked me, Drew!"

"Good for him." I roll my eyes. "Now go to bed."

Libby reluctantly leaves my room, blowing kisses to the rabbit the whole way out the door.

When she's gone, I get up and shut the closet door. "Good night, rabbit. We'll figure out what to do with you tomorrow."

Then I change into my pyjamas and go brush my teeth without Mom or Dad having to tell me. After the day I've had, I'm exhausted. I check the rabbit one more time before I head to bed. He's sleeping in the same corner he was before, his nose wiggling from time to time, and his mouth moving like he's chewing something in his dreams. Probably my computer cords.

I turn out the light and climb into bed. Just as I'm getting drowsy, Mom pokes her head in the door.

"You're in bed early."

I pretend I'm already fast asleep.

"I know you're awake, Drew." She sits on the side of my bed. For a long moment she doesn't say anything.

I roll over. "What?"

"You know your dad loves you right?"

"Yeah," I say. "I know."

"He's just worried."

"Worried about what?"

Mom sighs. "I know it's a lot to ask you to watch Libby every day after school. I wish I could be home like other moms. But right now, it's just not possible. You understand that, right?"

"Yeah, Mom. I know," I say, even though I'm totally confused. What does babysitting Libby have to do with Dad being worried? Why do parents always have to talk in riddles?

Mom doesn't say anything for a while. Then she leans over and kisses me, ruffles my hair, and gets up to leave the room. At the door she pauses. "I love you, Drew."

"I know."

"Good night."

"G'night." I burrow deeper under the covers. I try to puzzle through what Mom meant, but I can't stay awake any longer.

A few minutes later, I drift off to sleep.

THUMP!

Whatever I was dreaming of vanishes in an instant and I'm wide awake. What was that?

THUMP!

The sound is coming from the closet. That stupid rabbit!

Muttering to myself, I pull back the covers and tip-toe to the closet. I can barely make out the rabbit in the dark, but I can see his ears are bolt upright on his head. "What is it?"

THUMP!

The house is dead silent. Somewhere up the road, I can hear a car driving by, but there aren't any other sounds to be heard. "All right, that's enough now. You're gonna wake Mom and Dad. Then you'll have something to be afraid of." I run my hand down his back. He feels tense.

THUMP!

"Tiny, stop. It's okay." I rub the rabbit's forehead the way Libby does and he relaxes a bit. He lies down and lets me pet him for a few minutes. He seems to go back to sleep.

"See now, there's nothing to be afraid of. Go to sleep." I close the closet door and head back to bed. My head is barely on my pillow when . . .

THUMP!

"What am I going to do with you, rabbit?" I glance at the clock on my bed stand. It's one in the morning. With a sigh, I switch on my lamp, crawl out of bed and open the closet door.

The rabbit sits up on his back legs, his nose wiggling. Then he hops past me and begins sniffing my dresser, then my bed, and then my desk. "Uh-uh. No more computer cord eating tonight." I shoo him away from my desk. He hops over to the pile of comic books on the floor and nibbles the corner of one.

"No! No comic book eating either." I grab the comics and dump them on my desk. Dad's right: Rabbits do eat everything.

"So now what?" I ask. The rabbit stops and swivels an ear at me. I grab the comic I was reading—or trying to read—earlier, flip it open, and lie down on my bed.

All the rabbit does is hop and sniff, pausing every so often to stand on his back legs. After a while, and three issues of *Galactic Bounty Hunter*, I can barely keep my eyes open. I yawn.

"Okay, rabbit. Back in the closet. I gotta get some sleep." I herd the rabbit into the closet and shut the door. I climb back into bed, turn off the light, and . . .

THUMP!

I groan. "Don't you understand what sleep is, rabbit?" I'm tempted to wrap my pillow around my head and ignore him, but I know if he keeps it up much longer, he's bound to wake Mom and Dad.

I switch on the light, climb back out of bed again, and open the closet door. "What do you want?"

The rabbit regards me for a moment, wiggles its nose, and then hops back out of the closet. After he's thoroughly explored my bedroom, the rabbit does a funny jump: He hops straight up in the air and shakes his head, twisting his back legs out to the side. I laugh.

"What the heck was that?"

He gives me a disapproving look. Then he runs full speed around my room and does his funny little jump again, this time hip-checking my dresser in the process. He shakes his head and sits there for a moment, before taking off running again. At first it's kind of fun to watch, but after another ten minutes of him running dizzying circles, I lose interest.

I flop on my bed and stare at the ceiling. It's almost two in the morning and little bun-bun thinks it's playtime.

7
"Bad rabbit!"

When I wake up the next morning, I nearly have a heart attack. Looming over me is Libby in her nightgown. "Aw! Not fair!"

I sit bolt upright. "Don't do that! You nearly scared me to death."

It's barely light out. The glowing blue numbers on the clock on my bed stand say 5:05. Three hours' sleep. Little wonder I feel like road kill.

Libby points an accusing finger at me. "Not fair! You said Tiny couldn't sleep with me, but he's in bed sleeping with you."

"What?" I glance down. The rabbit is snuggled into a fold in my comforter. His right ear flicks towards Libby. Then he yawns and stretches and hops over to say hello.

I grit my teeth. "This is *not* what it looks like. I had *no* idea he was on my bed."

"I thought you said he had to stay in the closet?"

"He was thumping. I couldn't risk him waking up Mom and Dad, so I let him out."

The look on Libby's face could melt icebergs.

I rub my eyes. "What are you doing up so early anyway?"

"I wanted to see Tiny."

"And that couldn't wait till seven o'clock?"

Tiny is hopping around my bed, sniffing with interest. Suddenly, he squats, lifts his tail and pees.

"*No!* Bad rabbit!" I grab him and practically toss him off the bed. He lands on the floor, looks at me with mixture of shock and disgust, and hops into the closet, flicking his hind feet at me.

There's a huge puddle on my blue and white comforter.

"Quick! Run get a towel! Or two! Make it three!" I'm trying not to shout, but the huge puddle is spreading.

Libby runs for the door.

"*Quietly!*" I hiss.

A moment later, Libby returns with a pile of towels. I grab them from her, throw them onto the puddle of pee—and then realize these are Mom's brand new guest towels.

"Libby!"

So much for sleep.

I pull everything off my bed—sheets, comforter, wet towels and all—and sneak downstairs to the laundry room in the basement. For the first time in my life, I'm grateful Mom taught me how to use the washing machine. She got tired of me constantly bugging her to wash my gym strip and the never-ending notes that came home from Mr. Murray because I'd forgotten my strip at home.

"It's not rocket science," she'd said, showing me how to set the water level, temperature and wash setting.

Of course, once I knew how to wash my gym strip, I also found myself washing sheets and towels, underwear and socks, too. Mom says it's a big help. I say it's a violation of my human rights.

Once the wash is on, I grab a sleeping bag from the shelf above the washer and sneak upstairs to the kitchen to find something for the rabbit to eat. There's no lettuce left, so along with a couple carrots, I take a chance on some parsley and spinach.

Libby is playing with the rabbit when I get back to my room. He's hopping in and out of her lap. She giggles every time he hops into her lap. "His whiskers tickle."

I dump the vegetables into his dish. They barely touch the bottom before the rabbit's ears swivel in that direction like satellite dishes and he races into the closet to gobble them down. I shut the door. "Okay, Libby. It's time for you to go back to bed."

"But I'm not tired."

"Well, I *am*."

"I want to play with Tiny."

"Look, if Mom and Dad wake up, they're going to wonder what we're doing up at five thirty in the morning. You don't want to make them suspicious, do you?"

Libby pouts.

"Pretend to sleep, if you're not tired. Okay?"

Finally, I convince her to go back to her room.

Then I unroll the sleeping bag on my bed and climb into it. I'm asleep in seconds.

🥕   🥕   🥕

"Drew!" Mom's voice from the doorway snaps me back into wakefulness. "What are you still doing in bed? You're going to miss the bus."

"I'm up. I'm up," I mumble and drag myself from bed.

I check on the rabbit, who's asleep in the corner again, grab my clothes, homework, gym strip, and everything else I can think of. Then run downstairs to stuff a piece of toast into my mouth and grab my lunch bag.

The bus is waiting at the corner as Libby and I race out the door and down the road.

"You guys are cutting it close this morning," the bus driver says, closing the doors behind us as we climb aboard.

Libby goes to sit with one of her little friends and I'm free to claim a seat at the back all by myself, press play on my iPod, and try to catch a few more minutes of sleep.

The twenty-minute bus ride into town goes by much too quick, and we pull up outside the three-story red brick building that is Douglas Bay Elementary School. I go line up at my classroom door with the other students already gathered there.

"Hey, Drew!" Maya Fletcher, the most popular girl in grade six, points at my shoes. "Did you go colour blind last night?"

"What?" I glance down. I've got a black shoe on one foot and a brown shoe on the other. I groan.

"Maybe he thinks it's the new look?" Maya's best friend, Ally Henderson, smirks.

"Well, maybe it is the new look," I protest.

"Yeah, right." Maya rolls her eyes. "Maybe you need your mommy to put your shoes on for you."

Ever since the Papier-Mâché Incident in grade three Maya has always hated me. It wasn't like I did it on purpose. How was I supposed to see the chair blocking my path when I was carrying a brimming tray of papier-mâché?

"Shut up, Maya!" I say.

"Make me!"

I glare at her and wish Quentin would hurry up and get to school. Quentin always has the best comebacks and if anybody ever tries to bug us, he always turns things around on them so fast they feel like they're the ones being bugged instead. But Quentin isn't at school yet, and I can't think of a single smart thing to say. So for the next five minutes until the bell rings, Maya, Ally, and a couple of the other kids find about fifty different ways to ridicule me for wearing two different-coloured shoes to school.

Finally the bell goes, and I hurry after the rest of my class into the school to hang up my coat and backpack and change into my inside shoes—which at least match.

But as soon as I pull off my coat, Maya bursts out laughing. "Hey, Drew! Did you forget how to dress yourself this morning too?"

I glance down. Not only have I worn two different-coloured shoes, but my shirt is also on inside out *and* backwards. The tag is sticking out under my nose like a white flag.

Could this day get any worse?

It does. I'm so tired I fall asleep during math class. I'm dreaming I'm riding a giant caramel-coloured rabbit running full speed down a hill. Suddenly a gigantic dirt jump appears ahead of us. The rabbit tightens its muscles and leaps forward with such speed I lose my balance and tumble off backward.

I sit up with a gasp. It takes me a second to realize I'm at school. It takes another to realize there's a piece of paper stuck to my face with dried drool. I peel it off, hoping no one has noticed. But everyone in the class is looking at me.

"Nice of you to join us, Mr. Montgomery," Mr. Plonski says.

There are a few giggles.

At recess it's raining hard again, so we have to stay inside. Usually, the teachers kick us outside whether it's raining or not, but lately it's been raining so much they seem to feel sorry for us and let us stay in the classroom. At least I don't have to put my mismatched shoes back on.

Since Quentin is absent, I've got nobody to play cards with. Normally, this wouldn't be such a big deal, but I really need to talk to him. Instead, I spend the fifteen-minute break doodling a picture of Maya and Ally being eaten by sharks.

"Whatcha drawing?" Maya appears at my elbow.

"Nothing." I try to cover the picture.

Too late. Ally grabs it and she and Maya run shrieking across the classroom together to look at it.

"You are so dead, Drew Montgomery!" Maya crosses her arms.

"Wait! That's not you guys. That's my little sister and her annoying little friend."

"Oh sure. Since when do your little sister and her friend have shirts that say MAYA and ALLY?" Ally says.

"It's not you guys!" I insist. "Now, give it back."

"Make me!" Maya says.

"Yeah!" Ally says.

I grab for the picture, but Maya dodges behind a desk. "Nice try, Drew."

"Oh, come on." I reach across the desk, try to snatch it from her. But I lean too far and lose balance. Me, the desk, and Maya go tumbling to the ground.

Maya screams like I've just tried to murder her. "You jerk! You did that on purpose!"

"No! It was an accident!" I say.

"I'm telling Mr. Plonski," Ally says.

Too late.

So I end up with a detention and have to write apology letters to both Maya and Ally.

Next is gym class. When I pull out my gym strip in the change room, I realize there are a bunch of small holes nibbled into the fabric. That rabbit!

I yank on my shorts and take a peek at my rear end in the mirror. You can see my underwear right through the holes. Are you serious? I pull them off again, climb back into my clothes and go tell Mr. Murray, "I think I forgot my gym strip at home."

"Well, you know the drill. Better grab some out of the Lost and Found," he says.

I groan. What's worse? Wearing somebody else's sweaty gym strip for half an hour or parading around the gym in shorts so full of holes everyone can see my tighty-whities? Yeah, I think the answer's pretty obvious too.

I go grab the cleanest-smelling shorts and tee shirt from the Lost and Found in the hallway and hurry to change into them.

Can this day just end?

🥕 🥕 🥕

Finally, the bell rings and I get Libby from class and go catch our bus. She's signed out a book on rabbits from the school library: *The Ultimate House Rabbit Guide Book*. On the bus ride home, she seems to think I want to hear all about rabbits. Which I don't. I'd be quite happy if I never heard about the furry little monsters ever again.

Of course, with Libby sitting next to me, that isn't going to happen.

"Did you know rabbits' teeth never stop growing?" she says.

"That's really great, Libby."

"Wow! Rabbits sleep with their eyes open, too. How weird is that?"

"Very weird."

"Look! There's a bunny on a leash. I want to take Tiny for a walk, too."

"You go right ahead and do that."

"Aw! When rabbits jump in the air it's called a binky. That's so cute."

"Yeah, really cute."

"Oh, wow! Look at this big bunny. He's called a Flee-mish Guy-ant."

"That's—*a what*?" I glance over at the book. "That's 'Flemish Giant.'" There's a picture of a lady holding a large grey rabbit. And it's big. No, it's *huge*. I've never seen a bunny that big in my life. The thing is almost as big as Quentin's cocker spaniel, Barkley.

"Aw! Look at this bunny with the long ears. Aw! And this one with the spots. Oh, they're all so cute, Drew. What kind of bunny do you think Tiny is?" She shoves the book in my face.

"Oh, I don't know." I quickly scan the page, looking for the first rabbit that looks anything like Tiny. There's a picture of a small, caramel-coloured rabbit called a Mini Rex. I point it out. "This one looks kinda like him, don't you think?"

"Aw! He looks *just* like Tiny." Libby nods so enthusiastically she looks like a bobble head.

The bus pulls up to our stop, and we grab our backpacks, climb off, and march up the road to our house.

Inside, we dump our coats and backpacks and then hurry upstairs to my room.

"Yuck!" What is that smell?" Libby says.

I open the closet door and it's obvious. The doll's bed is completely soaked with rabbit pee and covered in a huge pile of poops. Man, this rabbit sure likes to pee on beds.

"Tiny!" Libby cries. "You wrecked your bed."

"Gross." I wrinkle my nose. "You better clean that up."

"I'm not touching it."

"You put it in there."

"To sleep on. Not to *pee* on."

"Libby!"

Finally we agree that I'll pick up the blanket and Libby will pick up the mattress. We get a garbage bag and dump as much of the poop into it as we can. Then we run downstairs and shove everything else into the washer.

"That animal is disgusting." I close the lid and set the dial to "heavy duty wash."

"He just needs a better bathroom," Libby says, pulling out the rabbit book and flipping to a page. She holds it up. "See. He needs a cat litter box. Like this one."

"And where are we going to get that?"

"The pet store."

"Do you know how much trouble we'll be in if we get caught sneaking off to the pet store?"

Libby's lower lip starts to tremble.

"No! There is no way—"

Suddenly she brightens. "I know!" She spins around and runs upstairs.

She's digging around in the cupboard next to the sink when I arrive in the kitchen.

"Aha!" She stands up, triumphant. In her hand is a large, rectangular plastic storage container. "This is just what we need."

We fill the container with shredded newspaper and put it in the corner where the doll bed used to be. Tiny hops over, sniffs the container, then hops inside and relieves himself.

And yet again, my sister is bordering on genius. But I'm not about to tell her that. I'd rather stick freshly sharpened pencils up my nose.

8
Crazy Rabbit!

There's an extra-large salad on the dinner table to-night.

"Just for Libby," says Mom.

Libby beams up at her, scooping an extra-large helping onto her plate.

"Must be a growth spurt," Dad says.

"Y'know, I thought Libby looked a bit taller today," I say, nodding.

Mom sighs. "Again? I just bought her new shoes."

Once dinner is finished, Libby and I hurry to clear the table. We scrape the plates and stack them in the dishwasher, then we head to the stairs and my room.

"Drew, aren't you forgetting something?" says Mom.

I turn back and quickly scan the table, but it's cleared

of every last fork and napkin. Only a few crumbs remain.

"I don't think so."

"Isn't tomorrow garbage and recycling day?"

Libby's already halfway up the stairs to my room. I can only imagine all the trouble she and that rabbit will get into in my room without me. My comic books. My computer. My iPod!

"Can't I take it out in the morning?"

Mom sets her hands on her hips.

"Okay, okay, I'll do it now."

It seems to take forever to empty the nine wastebaskets in our house—why we have so many is a mystery to me—plus sort all the cans, newspapers, glass, cardboard and plastics into the appropriate bins. I swear my family creates more recycling than any other family on the block. But I finally get everything emptied and sorted and dragged out to the curb for the trucks to take away in the morning. Then I race back inside.

"Did you remember the garbage in the laundry room?" Mom says as I bound up the stairs.

"Yes!" I call down to her, though I really did forget to empty it. It's not like it's going to overflow onto the floor in the next seven days.

"And the newspapers in Dad's office?"

"Yes!"

I throw open my door, but my room is empty. "Libby? Rabbit?"

I check the closet and under my bed. Then I hear a familiar squeal coming from Libby's room.

Dreading what I might discover, I rush down the hall to find Libby, dressed in her fanciest pink princess dress, having a tea party. The rabbit—which is, believe it or not, wearing a purple velvet cape and a silver crown—is standing on a toy chair, eating its salad off a small china plate on the toy table.

"What are you *doing*?"

"Having a tea party."

"Do you have any idea how much trouble you'd get into if Mom or Dad walked in right now?"

Libby pouts.

"The rabbit *has* to stay in my room. What if he decided to take off downstairs right now? What would you do?"

"He doesn't want to go downstairs. Do you, Tiny? You want to stay here and play with me."

The rabbit has finished his salad and hops off the chair, wriggling out of the velvet cape at the same time. He sits down in the corner and scratches the crown off with his back leg. He looks disapprovingly at me.

"Just get him back into my room. Now."

"Okay, okay." Libby grumbles, picks up the rabbit and carries him back into my room.

Great. *Now* he decides he likes being picked up.

"Libby, bedtime!" Mom calls upstairs. "Did you bring your library book home with you today?"

"Yes!"

"Well, hurry up and get your pyjamas on and your teeth brushed and we'll read it together, okay?"

Libby lets the rabbit go in my room and hurries off to the bathroom. I shut the door behind her and plop down on my computer chair.

The rabbit is sniffing a pile of dirty socks on the floor. He starts digging at them, then picks one up in his teeth and tosses it into the air.

"Hey, leave my socks alone!" I grab them and throw them into the hamper. Crazy rabbit!

Even though I'm really tired and should probably head to bed early tonight, I decide to check if Quentin is online. Maybe even give Alien Doom another shot. But first I lock the rabbit in the closet. Then I hit the power button on my computer.

Nothing. The lights don't come on. The fan doesn't start.

I punch the button again repeatedly. What the heck?

Then I glance under my desk.

I can barely believe it. Every *single* cord hanging down the back has been chewed in half. Some have even been chewed into two or three pieces.

That rabbit! I clench my fists and my jaw. Oh, what

I would do to that rabbit if it weren't for Libby and her blackmailing. It would be dead meat.

I stand up and stalk up and down my room. I can't believe I let my little sister blackmail me into keeping this stupid, computer-wrecking, bed-peeing rabbit. There's got to be a way out of it. But how? Unless . . . Unless I find out something Libby has done and blackmail her back. Something even bigger than my bike. Something so big she wouldn't ever dare say the word "bike" around Mom and Dad again. Then I could get rid of the rabbit.

Satisfied with my plan, I sit down on my bed.

Right in a puddle of rabbit pee.

🥕 🥕 🥕

For the second time today, I yank the sheets and comforter—the *freshly washed* sheets and comforter I *just* made my bed with—off and head for the laundry room.

As I'm about to go downstairs, I hear Mom and Libby reading in her room.

I tiptoe over to the door. Libby is tucked under her pink princess comforter, holding *The Ultimate House Rabbit Guide Book*. Mom is sitting beside her on the bed with her back to me.

"Aren't these the cutest little bunnies?" Libby says, holding the book up for Mom to see. "Look at this little bunny here. It's called a Mini Rex. Don't you think he's the cutest bunny ever?"

"Yes, he's pretty cute," Mom says, nodding.

"Wouldn't it be nice if we had a bunny like that?" Libby's got that look on her face again like she's about to ask for cookies or ice cream.

Mom's shoulders sag. "Libby, I know you kids would like a pet. But your father and I work full time. Who will take care of it and remember to feed it and exercise it and clean up after it?"

"I will. I promise I will. And Drew will help."

"And what about when we're at work and you're at school? Do you think it's fair to keep a pet at home all alone?"

I can see the look in Libby's eye. She's about to spill the beans.

"Hey, Mom," I interrupt. "Do you need any laundry done?"

Mom turns around to face me. "Oh, yes. As a matter of fact, I do. Hang on a sec." She glances at the bundle of sheets in my arms as she walks past me, into her room. "It's a bit late for washing sheets, isn't it?"

My face burns and I stammer, "I, uh, it's homework. We have to, uh, do some housework for, uh, Health and Careers."

"Well, you better get them into the washer. You need to get to bed soon."

As soon as Mom's out of sight, I give Libby a warning look. "Are you *trying* to get us in trouble?"

"I just thought . . ." Libby looks down at the book.

"Well, don't. You promised not to say a word, so don't!"

Mom returns with a huge armload of laundry. "Thanks, Drew, you're a big help."

Then she goes back into Libby's room, kisses Libby on the forehead and says, "We'll talk about this later, okay?"

I can hardly believe my ears. It's always been "*No! No! No!*" every time I've asked for a pet. And here Mom's going to "talk about it later"? That might as well be a "*Maybe.*" And a "*Maybe*" is halfway to a "*Yes!*"

"Gee, Mom. Can I have a dog?" I say.

Mom gives me a look that says, "Don't be ridiculous."

I roll my eyes and carry my mountain of laundry downstairs to the basement.

THUMP!

With a groan, I glance at the clock: 12:45. Not again.

THUMP!

I pull back the covers, switch on the light on my bed stand and go open the closet door.

The rabbit hops right out and starts sniffing around my room. As quick as I can, I grab my comic books, clothes, schoolwork, and my prized iPod off the floor, plop them on my desk, and crawl back into bed.

Pleased with my handiwork, I turn out the light. "Good night, rabbit."

THUMP!

Are you kidding me?

I switch the light back on. "What? Now I have to sleep with the light on too?"

9
Uh Oh!

For the second morning in a row, I wake up to find Libby's face hovering a few inches from mine. I nearly jump out of my pyjamas.

"Can't you knock?" I scrub the sleep from my eyes. At least the clock displays a much more reasonable hour: 6:51. Nine minutes before my alarm would usually go off.

"Why do you get to sleep with Tiny and I don't?"

I glance down. Just like yesterday, there is the rabbit, snuggled up next to my feet on the comforter. He yawns and stretches and starts sniffing around my bed.

"Oh, no you don't!" I pick him up and dump him on the floor. "Your litter box is in the closet. Not on my bed."

The rabbit gives me an offended look, but hops over to the closet and into the plastic bin.

Libby crosses her arms. "I want Tiny to sleep with me tonight."

"Believe me, this isn't planned. I had to let him out again. He was thumping. It's not like I actually *enjoy* sleeping with the rabbit." Okay, maybe that's not entirely true. It's kinda nice waking up with a warm little ball of fur tucked against your legs, but I'd sooner wear Mom's pink nail polish to school than tell Libby that.

"Why don't you go get the rabbit some breakfast?" I say.

"What are you going to do?"

"I'm going to get a few more minutes of sleep." I roll over and pull my pillow over my head.

Libby leaves the room, closing the door behind her.

I'm just drifting off to blissful sleep again when . . . *BEEP! BEEP! BEEP!*

Reaching out blindly, I try to hit the snooze button, but only manage to knock my alarm clock onto the floor. Now the clock is somewhere under my bed and still wailing away. *BEEP! BEEP! BEEP!* I roll over, drag it out and turn it off.

Libby reappears. "What are you doing hanging halfway out of bed?"

"Nothing." I put my clock back on the bed stand and roll back into bed. "Where's the lettuce?"

"Dad came downstairs while I was getting the bag out of the fridge."

"He what?" I sit bolt upright. "What did he say?"

"That no matter how much I like salad now, I'm not eating it for breakfast."

I exhale with relief.

"So what about the rabbit?"

Libby pulls a handful of Cheerios from her pocket.

"Cheerios? He's not going to eat Cheerios."

Libby pours them into his dish and the rabbit hops over and, to my amazement, starts crunching away. Libby sits down beside the rabbit and strokes his nose. "The book says bunnies can have Cheerios as a treat. We can sneak him some lettuce later."

🥕 🥕 🥕

"Drew, you look tired," Mom says, setting a piece of toast spread with peanut butter in front of me. "Did you sleep okay last night?"

"I, uh, yeah, I slept fine."

"Well, I didn't sleep so great last night," Dad says with a yawn, walking into the kitchen and dropping his suit jacket over the back of his chair. He gives Mom a kiss on the cheek. "I swore I heard thumping last night."

"I thought I heard it too." Mom nods. "And the night before."

Uh oh! "Well, I didn't hear anything." I glance at Libby. "What about you? Did you hear any thumping?"

"Nope." She sets her glass of milk on the table, licking the milk moustache on her upper lip.

Mom hands her a napkin. "What do you think it was, Todd?"

"Hey, Mom, do we have any honey?" I say, trying to change the subject.

"In the pantry," Mom says, waving her hand in that direction.

"I honestly haven't a clue what it was," Dad says. "Maybe the furnace? Or the hot water tank?"

"Oh, I hope not. We had them both serviced in the fall," Mom says.

Dad shrugs. "Your guess is as good as mine, Jess."

I open the pantry and pull out the BeeMaid container, then sit down again to spread some honey over top of the peanut butter on my toast.

"Would you close the pantry, Drew?" Mom sets her hands on her hips. "You kids are forever leaving the door open!"

"Sorry," I mumble through a mouthful of toast and get up to close the pantry door.

"Whatever it is," Dad says, "if I hear it again, I'll be sure to check it out."

I glance over at Libby. She's looking at me, eyes round as moons. Uh oh!

Quentin is still absent from school. Mr. Plonski says he has chicken pox and we have to take home a notice about it. He might be absent for a week or even longer. A week! I can barely survive a day without Quentin. How am I going to survive a whole week?

At lunch, I have to stay in the classroom to serve my detention, while the rest of the kids get to go outside and play. I spend the time working on my apology letter:

Dear Maya and Ally,

I'm sorry I accidentally knocked my desk over on you and you thought I did it on purpose. This wouldn't have happened if I hadn't drawn a picture of you being eaten by sharks. Now that I've had some time to think about it, I think I would have rather drawn a picture of you buried up to your necks in sand, surrounded by deadly fire ants.

What I have learned from this experience is that if I ever want to draw pictures of my classmates dying painful deaths, I should do it at home so I can pin the picture to the corkboard in my bedroom and admire it any time I want.

Sincerely,
Drew Montgomery

But then I decide I don't want to be in detention till the end of grade six. So I crumple up that letter and start over:

Dear Maya and Ally,
    I'm sorry I accidentally knocked my desk over on you and you thought I did it on purpose. This wouldn't have happened if I hadn't drawn a picture of you being eaten by sharks. I know it is inappropriate to draw pictures of your classmates dying painful deaths. I won't ever draw pictures like that at school again. I will also be more careful with my desk.
    Sincerely,
    Drew Montgomery

Once I've finished my letter, I still have a few minutes before lunch ends, so I get out another piece of paper and draw a picture of Maya and Ally buried up to their necks in sand, surrounded by deadly fire ants. For good measure, I throw in some hungry alligators, too. Then I carefully fold up my picture and put it in my pocket. When Mr. Plonski comes in, he seems satisfied with my letter and I am freed from detention.

As I head outside to the playground, I decide the first thing I'm going to do when I get home is pin my new picture to the corkboard in my bedroom.

On the bus ride home, Libby tells me she's come up with an idea to keep the rabbit from thumping. I'd spent a few minutes of my detention trying to come up with an idea myself, but the only thing I could think of was: *Get rid of the rabbit!* And since I still haven't got anything to blackmail Libby with, I guess I'm stuck with the rabbit.

The bus drops us off and we race home, dump our coats and backpacks, phone Mom, and hurry upstairs to my room.

Tiny is in his usual spot, fast asleep in the corner of the closet.

"So what's this great plan of yours?" I ask.

"You'll see," Libby says and heads off downstairs.

I take a moment to pin the picture of Maya and Ally to the corkboard above my desk, admire it with satisfaction, and then follow Libby to the basement.

She's struggling to pull the old baby gate—the one Mom has kept around for when Aunt Leila and Uncle Justin bring baby Ethan to visit—from behind a stack of plastic bins.

"Hang on." With a grunt, I shove the bins aside and Libby pulls the baby gate free.

Libby claps her hands. "Now help me carry it upstairs!"

We take it back to my room and with a bit of work manage to fit it into the door jamb in my closet. Tiny hops over right away to sniff it. He stands on his back legs, pressing his front paws to the mesh on the baby gate, and gives us his saddest look. As I swing the door shut and latch it, a grin spreads across my face.

I've got my room back.

"Libby, you're a—" I clamp my mouth shut. I can't believe what I almost said. I'd rather swim in radioactive sludge than tell my sister she's a genius. "Um, yeah, that should keep him in all right."

Libby grins back at me. "I've got another idea, too!" She disappears into her room. A moment later, she returns with her unicorn nightlight. She plugs it into the outlet next to the closet. "Now Tiny won't have to be scared at night."

"What about you? Won't you be scared without your nightlight?"

She shakes her head. "Oh no, I won't be scared at all."

The next morning, I wake up to Libby's face, yet again, barely inches away from mine. Only this time, she's not hovering over my bed, she's *in* my bed, fast asleep.

"Libby!"

Her eyes blink open.

"What are you doing in my bed?"

"I was scared last night."

"And you couldn't go cuddle with Mom and Dad?"

"Oh no! Then I'd have had to tell them where my nightlight was."

I groan and roll over. Then I notice the rabbit, curled up between us, at the bottom of the bed.

"How did he get out?"

"He was scared too."

I flop back on my pillow. Was I ever going to get a good night's sleep?

10
Blackmail

At breakfast, there's no mention of thumping from either Mom or Dad. Hopefully, this means they're going to forget about it.

On the bus ride to school, I decide I need to talk to Libby about the whole sleeping situation.

"Listen," I whisper. "You're going to have to get your own nightlight."

"But I already have a nightlight," Libby says in a much too loud voice. "It's in your room."

"Would you keep your voice down? Do you want the whole bus to hear you?" I glance around nervously, but no one seems to have heard. Everyone is busy talking and laughing and eating and scribbling in notebooks and listening to music.

"Look, what I mean is, we'll have to get you *another*

nightlight. One for your room. One for mine. You can even have your unicorn light back if you want."

"Can't I sleep with Tiny in my bed? I wouldn't be scared then."

"No. Absolutely not." I shake my head. "The rabbit stays in my room."

"But you keep saying you won't sleep with him in your bed, but then you do!"

"Be quiet! Please!" I glance around again. But there's not one smug smirk from the other kids, not a single snort of laughter. "Look, he's staying in the closet tonight. Understand? Now that I've got the baby gate and the nightlight, I don't have to let him out. Okay?"

She crosses her arms and pouts, but she doesn't say any more.

It's the third day Quentin is absent from school and I'm really beginning to miss him. As we file into the school, Maya leans over and whispers, "I see your shoes are matching today. Did your mommy help you dress yourself?"

Oh, Quentin, where are you?

In science, Mr. Plonski announces we're going to be starting a project on renewable energy sources. "Everyone pick a partner."

Normally, Quentin and I would partner up right away. But since he's away, I've got to find somebody else. I scan the room. Already Matt and Levi, Owen and Tanner, Derek and Aiden have paired up. There's a tap on my shoulder. I glance up. Tabitha Schaeffer towers over me. "Want to be my partner?"

"I, um . . ." It's not that I don't want to be partners with Tabitha, it's just that, well, I don't want to be partners with Tabitha. I'm sure she's a nice girl. But that's just it: she's a *girl*. And not only that, she's weird. None of the other girls like her. She wears a man's tie to school. Every day. And those old-fashioned black-and-white shoes that look like old police cars. Like plain old jeans and a tee shirt aren't good enough for her? Plus she's huge. She's taller than all the guys in grade six. And could probably twist half of them into a pretzel. While that's great in gym class, I'm not so sure that's much help for a science project.

"All right. It looks like everyone's got a partner," Mr. Plonski says.

Wait! What? I don't have a partner. I put up my hand.

"Yes, Drew?"

"What about Quentin?"

"Well, he'll just have to work with Michaela, since they're both absent today."

I drop my hand and slump in my desk. I don't want

Quentin to be partners with Michaela. I want Quentin to be partners with me.

"Anyway, since you've had your hand up, Drew, you and Tabitha can work on geothermal energy." Then Mr. Plonski assigns each set of partners an energy source for their project.

Maya glances over at me and whispers something into Ally's ear. Ally giggles and looks at me.

"Also," says Mr. Plonski, "there will not be a lot of class time allotted for research. You'll need to do that on your own time."

I groan.

At recess, the guys give me a hard time when I come to play soccer with them. "Why don't you go play with the girls?" Derek says.

"Yeah," says Tanner. "Where's your new girlfriend, Tabitha?"

"She's not my girlfriend!"

"Drew and Tabitha sitting in a tree, K-I-S-S-I-N-G!" Aiden says in a sing-songy voice and all the guys start laughing.

"Forget it," I say. "Who wants to play with a bunch of jerks anyway?"

"Hey, we're just joking around," Aiden says.

But I'm already marching off to the playground. Maybe someone wants to play grounders. I find the girls huddled underneath the slide, whispering. Ally glances in my direction and smirks. Then all the girls look over and start giggling.

I give up on grounders and go sign out a soccer ball from the gym. I spend recess kicking the ball against the side of the school by myself. "Darn you rabbit and Maya and Ally and Mr. Plonski and Tabitha, too," I mutter.

I wind up and kick the ball as hard as I can. It rebounds off the wall and out into the playground. Before I can say or do anything, it hits the playground supervisor in the back of the head.

"Oof!" She turns around, rubbing the spot the ball hit. "Drew, would you put the ball away and go find something else to do?"

As I head back to the gym with my ball, I really miss Quentin.

And I really, really miss Quentin when recess ends and I walk into the classroom and read the large black letters written on the whiteboard: *DREW MONTGOMERY STILL SLEEPS WITH A BUNNY STUFFIE AND A NIGHTLIGHT!* Around the words are drawings of babies in diapers with giant pacifiers.

My face burns so hot, I think my ears might spontaneously combust.

A few giggles break out across the room.

Then Mr. Plonski spots the whiteboard. "Who's responsible for this?" He grabs an eraser and scrubs it off, but I can still faintly read the words like they're permanently burned into the white background.

No one says a word.

"Maya? Ally? Do you know anything about this?"

"No, Mr. Plonski. Not me," Maya says, her eyes widening.

Ally shakes her head. "Me either."

He frowns. "Well, ladies, I'm not sure I believe you. We will discuss this in my office at lunch."

"Yes, Mr. Plonski," Maya mumbles.

Ally looks down at her science book.

But the moment his back is turned, the two of them turn on me, glaring.

"Nice try, Drew," Maya whispers. "Do you think we're stupid?"

"We know you did it!" Ally adds. "You're so dead meat!"

I slump in my desk. I hate girls. Almost as much as I hate rabbits.

🥕　🥕　🥕

After school, Libby wants to take the rabbit into the backyard.

"What for?" I ask.

"The book says rabbits need ack—ack—"

I take the book from her. "'Access to unlimited hay.'

Hay? It's a rabbit, not a horse. Where are we going to get hay?"

"Hay is *grass*, dummy!" Libby scowls at me.

I glare right back. "I know *that*. And I'm not a dummy." I'm about to say, "And no, you can't go in the backyard. What if he runs away? Or gets lost?" But then I realize if he runs away or gets lost, then he's not my problem anymore. "Sure thing, Libby. Feed him as much grass as he can eat."

So Libby takes the rabbit and a blanket and her teddy bears and dolls and sets up a picnic for them outside.

As soon as the back door closes, I head straight for the phone.

I call Quentin's house. His mother answers.

"Hi, Mrs. Chow. Is Quentin there?"

"I'm sorry, Drew, Quentin's asleep right now."

"Oh. Well, can you get him to call me later?"

"If he's feeling up to it. I'll tell him you called."

I hang up the phone and stare at the floor. Just when I need Quentin most. I was really counting on him for advice. Looks like I'm on my own with this one.

In my room, I get my great-grandpa's old grey hat—the same kind my dad says James Bond wears—off the top shelf in my closet and put it on along with a pair of sunglasses. Then I grab my camera and my Super-Sleuth Spy Kit and tiptoe down the hall into Libby's room.

I'm not exactly sure what I'm looking for. Just some-thing—anything—I can use against her. I hunt through her dresser drawers, then her desk, and finally lift up her mattress and check underneath. Nothing.

There's got to be *something* I can use.

I glance around her room. What's left? Just her closet and her bookcase. I check the bookcase. Would you believe it? Her *diary* is sitting on the second shelf between a bunch of Animal Ark books and the Boxcar Children. My hands are trembling as I pull the pink and white book from the shelf. It says "My First Dia-ry" on the cover and has a large gold lock, with the key hanging from a gold chain attached to it. How conve-nient is that?

My heart beats faster. If a girl had any dark secrets, this would be the place to find them.

I open the lock and start reading:

Dear Diary,

I am so hapy that you are My Diary. I will keep you all ways and rite in you everey day.

Okay, not exactly the dirt I was hoping for. I keep going:

Dear Diary,

Today I went shoping with Mommy and got Choclat

Chip Cookys and Drew did'nt get any becus he did'nt
whant to come.

Oh, come on! There's got to be something better
than this. I skim the next few entries. It's all the same
garbage:

Dear Diary,
   I wish I was Cinedrella and had mise and birds
that wuld sow me a Beatifal Gowne to. And a wite
horse that culd talk to me.

Dear Diary,
   Today, I playde prinsesses with Katelyn. She put on
the Pink Gowne and I put on the Perpl Gowne and Mr
Wuzzy and Foofensnozle were the prinses.

Dear Diary,
   Today I thot waht fun it wuld be if insted of driving
cars, we went evereywere in Bubbels. And ate Cup-
kakes for brekfest. But mostly I whant the new Fary
Prinsess Barbie.

Blah, blah, blah. After another three or four pages
of the exact same stupid stuff, there are no more entries. No wonder she keeps it on her bookshelf with the
key attached. There's nothing in this so-called diary

that would even come close to getting her into trouble. Disgusted, I stuff the diary back onto the shelf.

Next I snap a picture of under her bed. There's a stray sock and a whole bunch of dust, but nothing else. I delete the picture. It's blurry anyway.

I take pictures of the closet. But it's just full of toys and dresses. Lots of dresses. No secrets there.

With a sigh, I plop down on her bed. This isn't going to work. There is absolutely nothing in this bedroom I can use against her. I'm about to give up hope of ever getting rid of that rabbit, then an idea hits me. A really great idea.

This is so perfect!

I hurry back to my room, grab a piece of paper and start scribbling. Time for Plan B!

When I am finished, I hold up my masterpiece. I've drawn a stick figure that sort of looks like me, with the words '*Drew is a big . . .*' and every single bad word I can think of—and even a few that I'm not sure if they're bad words or not but sound like they could be—written underneath. Every letter I've carefully copied from Libby's diary. I can just imagine the look on Mom and Dad's face when they see it.

If Libby won't do anything to get herself into trouble, I'll just have to do it for her. All I have to do is threaten to leave this somewhere for Mom and Dad to find and Libby will have no choice: That rabbit is history.

11
Plan B

D rew! Drew!" Libby calls from downstairs.

Is that a hint of panic in her voice? Has the rabbit escaped? Did an eagle swoop out of the sky and carry it off?

"Come see what Tiny is doing. Aw! He's so cute."

If only I should be so lucky.

With a sigh, I tuck the blackmail picture between the pages of one of the comics sitting on my desk and go downstairs to see what the excitement is all about. The rabbit is racing around the yard, jumping into the air and kicking its legs just like it did that first night in my bedroom. What did Libby call it? A binky. Libby is jumping up and down and clapping her hands with delight.

"Isn't he cute?"

"Yeah, Libby, very cute."

The rabbit stops running and stands on his back legs, wiggling his nose at me.

"Has he eaten enough grass yet? We need to get him inside before Mom and Dad get home. And we still have to do our homework."

"I don't have any homework," Libby says.

"Well, I do. So bring the rabbit back inside."

Tiny, of course, does not want to be caught. He ducks behind Mom's rosebush and won't come out.

Not again.

"Quick! Pick some dandelions!"

Libby starts plucking dandelions, but when I offer them to Tiny, he just sniffs at the leaves and squeezes further behind the bush.

"Come on out now, little bunny," I say in my best Libby voice, "before I kill you."

"Don't say that!"

"Okay, little bunny, come out before I get the neighbours' cat and *he* can kill you."

"*Drew!*" Libby's voice has reached the pitch where glass is in danger of shattering.

"Okay, okay. Easy on the eardrums!"

The rabbit crouches at the back of the bush, with a very displeased look on his face.

"Would you just come out already, you stupid rabbit?" If I try to squeeze behind the rose bush, I'm going to get ripped to shreds. But I don't see what other choice I have.

Just then Libby says, "I have an idea!"

"What?" At that moment, I'd take any idea that didn't involve my bare arms and those rose thorns.

"Hold on." She runs into the house. A moment later she comes back carrying a banana.

"A banana? Rabbits don't eat bananas. *Monkeys* eat bananas."

She peels the banana and holds it out to the rabbit.

He sniffs eagerly, takes a cautious step forward, then another.

"Come here, Tiny," Libby says. "Come get the nummy banana."

Soon enough the rabbit is hopping after Libby and the banana, right into the house, up the stairs, and into my bedroom. She breaks off a piece of banana and puts it in his dish. He gobbles it up, his whole body twitching all over.

"He twitches because he likes it," Libby says.

"Lemme guess," I say. "The book says rabbits can eat bananas?"

Libby grins and nods.

My sister is, once again, sounding like Einstein Junior. Not that I'd tell her that. I'd rather stick a fork in an electrical socket.

Just then, the back door slams.

"Drew? Libby?" Dad calls from downstairs.

Dad's home already? I check the time and my heart pounds. It's after five o'clock! Where did the afternoon go?

"Quick! Put the baby gate back up!"

Libby and I struggle to jam the gate back into the closet door and race downstairs to the kitchen.

"That's quite the mess you've left in the backyard, Libby," Dad says. "Better clean it up before it starts to rain again."

"Yes, Daddy," Libby says and scurries out to the backyard.

"What about you? Have you got your homework done?"

I stare at the tiles on the floor. "Um, no."

"What have you two been doing all day?"

I stare at my socks. I've got a hole started in my left toe. "Um, nothing."

Dad sighs. "Just get it done, Drew."

I run off to get my homework.

"Where are the Brussels sprouts?" Mom is rummaging through the drawers in the bottom of the fridge. "I could've sworn I bought Brussels sprouts the last time I went to the grocery store."

So far that rabbit has saved us from eating spinach, broccoli, asparagus, and now Brussels sprouts. I fed him the last one for breakfast. But I'd rather eat those Brussels sprouts with liver and onions than admit that rabbit has done me a favour. Least of all to Libby.

"I haven't seen any Brussels sprouts," I say.

"Well, that's just the strangest thing." Mom straightens up. "I was quite sure I bought some."

"Maybe you dreamed it?"

Mom frowns, then laughs. "I've had such a stressful week at work. Maybe I did."

At dinner, Libby wants to know if she and Mom can talk some more. "Y'know, about the book we were reading? The one about rabbits?"

Mom glances at Dad.

"Actually, Mom and I discussed it." Dad sets down his fork and squeezes Libby's shoulder. "But we'll talk more about it after dinner."

Beaming, Libby takes an extra-extra-large helping of salad.

That "*maybe*" is looking like a "*yes.*" This is so unfair. I've been asking Dad and Mom for a dog for as long as I can remember and it's always been "*No!*" but Libby asks for a bunny just once and she's gonna get it. I stare at my plate. Might as well have been Brussels sprouts. I'm not hungry anymore.

Once dinner is finished and the dishes cleared away, Mom reappears in the dining room with something behind her back. I can't tell for sure, but I think it's a large gift bag.

"Well, I decided to talk to Dad about it, Libby, and we've made a decision." Mom produces a small, caramel-coloured plush rabbit with a pink bow around its neck from the gift bag and hands it to Libby.

"I know it's not a real bunny," Dad says. "But we can't have a pet right now. Maybe in a few years, okay, honey?"

Libby looks heartbroken.

I, on the other hand, have not been so relieved in my life. What did Libby think she was going to do? Pull the rabbit out of the closet as soon as Mom and Dad gave their okay? "Oh, thank you for saying I could get a bunny, Mommy and Daddy. See, I've already got one right here. You don't even have to buy him!" Like that would've gone over well.

"Aw! Look at how little he is, Libby," I say. "You can call him Tiny."

Libby looks daggers at me. "You're not funny, Drew!" She looks like she's about to cry. For a millisecond I almost feel bad.

"Drew!" Mom gives me that tired look. "Don't you have anything better to do?"

Whatever. I stalk off to my room.

The rabbit is sitting on my bed. Beside him is a large puddle of pee.

"What the—? How did—?"

The baby gate is propped at an awkward angle in the closet door, a wide opening gaping at the bottom. In our hurry, Libby and I must not have got it in the door straight.

"Get off!" I chase the rabbit off my bed, but instead of hopping back into the closet, it scoots underneath the bed.

"Stupid rabbit." With a sigh, I start stripping my bed—again.

Then I spot my comic books. Somehow, that rabbit has got up onto my desk and now every last issue I own is lying in a heap on the floor—half of them in shreds. In amongst the shredded paper, I can make out bits of the blackmail picture I planned to use against Libby.

"*Where are you?*" In an instant, I'm down on all fours, searching under my bed. "I could wring your furry little neck, you long-eared rat!"

The rabbit sits in the far corner, glaring at me.

"Get out of there! Now!" I grab my hockey stick from behind my door and stab at the rabbit with it. It pops out from under the bed and runs out the door into the hallway.

No! I'd forgotten to close my bedroom door. I chase after the rabbit. It heads straight for Libby's room. As if that will do it any good. When I get my hands on that rabbit, it's dead meat.

The rabbit is hiding under Libby's bed, giving me a dirty look. I hate this rabbit so much. If Libby hated it half as much as I did she'd never want to—suddenly, an idea hits me.

I grab Libby's favourite doll, her favourite teddy bear, her favourite princess dress and dress up shoes, and her diary, and stuff them under the bed with the rabbit.

"Have fun," I say and leave the room, closing the door firmly behind me.

Then I finish stripping my bed, put on the laundry, go grab myself a snack from the kitchen, and sit down to watch some TV with Mom and Dad.

12
Revenge

Thursday nights, Libby is allowed to stay up late and watch TV with Mom and Dad and me. By nine o'clock, I've all but forgotten about the rabbit. But when Dad says, "Isn't it your bedtime, you two?" I suddenly remember and almost burst into maniacal laughter. I can't wait to see Libby's face when she walks into her room and sees the destruction.

Libby is snuggled sleepily against Mom, holding her new stuffed rabbit, Tiny Junior.

"C'mon, kiddo," Mom says, lifting Libby into her arms, and heads for the stairs.

Oh no! My mind races. Mom can't go upstairs. I have to stop her!

"Um, I can carry her if you want," I say.

Mom looks at me like I've grown two heads. "I think

I can manage, Drew."

"But . . ."

"But what?"

I don't know what to say. "Nothing."

All I can do is trudge up the stairs behind Mom and meet my doom. I try to think of what I'll say when she finds the rabbit:

"What rabbit? I don't see any rabbit."

Or maybe:

"Libby, I *told* you not to leave the back door open after school."

Or what about:

"It's just like the story *The Velveteen Rabbit*. Look! Tiny Junior has transformed into a real live rabbit!"

At any rate, this was all Libby's idea anyway. She can take one hundred percent of the blame. I'm not getting pinned with any of it.

Mom opens Libby's bedroom door and carries her inside. I stand in the hallway, just outside my own room, waiting for the yelling to start. But nothing happens. A few minutes later, Mom reappears in the hallway and quietly closes Libby's door behind her.

"What?" she says. Now she's looking at me like I've grown three heads.

"Nothing." I go into my room and sit down on my bed. What just happened there?

Mom sticks her head into my room. "Good lord, Drew, what a mess!" Her gaze sweeps over the growing pile of clutter on my desk and dresser tops, and the pile of shredded comics right in the middle of my floor. "What is that smell? It smells like a barn in here. Is that your gym strip?"

"I, um, I guess?"

"And where are your sheets?"

"I, uh, they're in the wash?"

"Well, I think you're going to be spending this weekend cleaning."

I stare at my hands. "Yes, Mom."

As soon as she goes back downstairs, I breathe again. Then I grab the flashlight out of the drawer in my bed stand, and sneak into Libby's room. She's tucked in her bed, fast asleep.

I flick on the flashlight and shine it under her bed. There's the rabbit, snuggled up between Libby's princess dress and the teddy bear, fast asleep. The rabbit blinks at the light and sits up. Then he yawns and stretches and sets to work washing the teddy bear's ears. The carnage doesn't look like much from here, so I pull Libby's things out one at a time, for a closer inspection. But I can't believe it. Not one of them has been chewed or peed on. Not the dress, the shoes, or the diary. Not even so much as any teeth marks. Unbelievable!

The rabbit has finished bathing the teddy bear and has flopped down beside it. I grab the teddy bear and yank it out. The rabbit sits up and gives me a very displeased look.

"You want your little furry buddy?" I whisper. "Then get back in the closet."

The rabbit stares at me for a few seconds, and then it hops out from under the bed.

I scoop it up before it can run and carry both it and the teddy bear to my bedroom and lock them both in my closet.

🥕   🥕   🥕

"Mr. Wuzzy!" Libby's shrill voice wakes me the next morning.

It would be so nice, just for one morning, not to wake up to Libby in my bedroom. I flop onto my back and stare at the ceiling. Then I remember the teddy bear. I sit up, imagining what the rabbit has done to it overnight: mounds of stuffing cover the closet floor—all that's left of the bear. "Is something wrong with Mr. Wuzzy?"

"No." Libby gives me a look like I've gone crazy. "Mr. Wuzzy and Tiny are just so cute. Aw! Tiny's licking Mr. Wuzzy's ears. Aw! Come look!"

I groan and roll over. "Yeah, Libby. Really cute. Seen it before."

After Libby leaves the room, I lie in bed, staring at the wall. I'm dreading school today. I can only imagine what revenge Maya and Ally have in store for me. Chewing gum on my seat, my clothes stolen during gym class, my lunch kit squashed, love letters that I'm supposed to have written being passed around, anything at all to do with permanent marker. I feel sick just thinking about it.

"Drew! What are you still doing in bed?" Mom says from my door.

"I don't feel so good," I say weakly.

Mom comes into the room and sits on my bed. "What's wrong?"

I shiver, like I've just been struck by chills. "I think I've got the chicken pox."

"You can't have the chicken pox. You had the shot when you were in kindergarten."

Oh. I cough feebly. "I have a sore throat. And a headache."

Mom feels my forehead. "Hmmm... Well, you don't seem to have a fever."

"I really don't feel good. I have a stomach ache too."

Libby appears at the door. "What's wrong with Drew?"

"He says he's sick. Could you bring me the Buckley's, please?"

Not the Buckley's! I let out a miserable moan.

Libby returns a moment later with the big bottle of cough and cold medicine and hands it to Mom.

"All right, Drew, this should make you feel better," Mom says, pouring out a dose of the medicine. "Open up."

I debate choking the disgusting medicine down, but I just can't bring myself to do it. That stuff is awful! "Y'know, I think I'm feeling a bit better," I say, sitting up.

My heart thumps as I realize the closet door is sitting wide open and all Mom has to do is glance in that direction and she'll see the rabbit. I raise my eyebrows at Libby and nod towards the closet. She looks confused a moment, then she quietly closes the closet and leaves the room.

Mom pours the medicine back into the bottle. "Good. Because you know I can't take off time from work to stay home and take care of you." She grabs a pair of jeans and a tee shirt out of the dresser and drops them on the bed beside me. "Now hurry up and get dressed. You don't want to miss the bus."

All through breakfast, I try to think of a way to get out of going to school. But I can't come up with anything. So at eight o'clock, Libby and I head out into the rain to the bus stop.

While Libby and I wait for the bus, I can't stop thinking about what Maya and Ally are going to do to me. Then a thought hits me: The only way to save myself from Maya and Ally's revenge is to find the guilty person and expose them. Then Maya and Ally will exact their revenge on them and not me.

There are five kids in my class who ride the same bus as me. Two are boys: Josh Macdonald and Toby Neville. Three are girls: Raina Novak, Willow Dawson, and Tabitha Schaeffer. One of them had to have overheard Libby and me talking. With the way the girls were whispering to each other on the playground and looking at me yesterday, I think it's pretty safe to rule out the guys. The culprit has to be one of the girls.

Tabitha, as usual, is sitting by herself towards the back of the bus, staring out what part of the window hasn't steamed up. Willow and Raina are sitting together, talking and giggling, as I climb aboard the bus. They stop talking as soon as they spot me, turning to gawk at me like I'm some kind of freak show as I walk past them. Definitely guilty.

I slide into the seat behind them.

"Hey, how's it going?" I say, trying to sound casual.

Willow and Raina ignore me and go back to whispering and giggling, their heads almost touching.

This isn't going well.

I try again. "I know who wrote my name on the whiteboard."

Willow spins around. "Who?"

"Oh, I think you know."

"Um, *no-o*, I *don't!*" She rolls her eyes at me.

I roll my eyes back at her. "Whatever you don't!"

"Drew, you are so weird," Raina says.

Willow sticks her tongue out at me.

Both girls turn around and neither of them will pay any more attention to me after that. No matter what I say. Or do.

Whatever. I crank up the volume on my iPod and stare straight ahead till we get to school.

At school, Maya and Ally act like I've turned invisible. They won't even look in my direction. This can't be good.

When I get into class, I check my desk, and then my chair. Nothing. I catch Maya and Ally giggling behind their hands. This is going to be a very long day.

Nothing happens during math and social studies. No notes are passed. No love letters signed with my name appear. The rest of the class seems as restless as I am, waiting for the nuclear bomb to go off.

But it doesn't.

At recess, I try again to figure out who wrote on the whiteboard. I catch Olivia, Willow and Raina's side-kick, coming out of the girls' washroom.

"I know who did it," I say.

"Did what?" Olivia's eyes narrow.

"Wrote my name on the board."

She takes a step back. "Well, it wasn't me!"

"Oh, I know that. But Willow and Raina better

watch their backs. I'm onto them!"

"Willow? Raina? What are you talking about?"

"Oh, I know it was them. They ride the bus with me and they must have heard me talking about—" I catch myself just in time. "My, um, sister's problem." My ears burn.

Olivia is looking at me like she's thinking of calling the mental institute because I've gone insane.

"Oh, never mind," I say and stomp off to the playground.

Maya and Ally serve their detentions at lunchtime and I'm free to play soccer with the guys again. That is, until Tabitha comes out to the field to watch.

"Hey, Drew, your girlfriend's here!" Tanner calls.

I clench my teeth and kick the ball so hard it flies past Tanner, through the goal posts, and bounces all the way into the playground. Tanner just ends up with grass stains on his jeans.

"Woo hoo! Nice goal!" Matt yells.

Aiden gives me a high-five.

During gym class, just to be safe, I stuff my clothes into Quentin's gym bag, making sure no one sees me do it. When I return to the change room, my gym bag is lying on the floor, my gym strip—my rabbit-chewed, holey gym strip—pulled out and trampled. Quentin's bag, on the other hand, is untouched. *Is that the best they can do?* I think, as I pull off Quentin's gym strip and climb back into my clothes.

The only other major blip of the day is during art class when Tabitha brings up our project.

"I was thinking we should get together to work on it this weekend," she says.

Just the words "get together" give me the hee-bie-jeebies.

There's a snort from Maya and Ally's direction. I try not to give them the satisfaction of looking over, but my glance slides that way anyway. They're both gawk-ing at me and smirking behind their hands.

My face heats up. "Yeah, uh, sure."

"Do you want me to come to your house or do you want to come over to mine?"

Another snort. And a giggle.

My heart hammers. Tabitha can't come to my house. And I'd rather roll in poison ivy than go to hers. "Um, how about the library? My computer's broken anyway."

"Okay. Are you doing anything after lunch tomor-row?"

"Um, I can't say for sure. I think I have to clean my room."

"Well, how about I call you tomorrow and we'll pick a time?"

I want to crawl under my desk and die.

13
Rats!

The bus drops us at the top of our road and Libby and I head home. I'm grateful it's Friday and I won't have to face Maya or Ally or any of my other classmates till Monday. Well, except Tabitha, who I'll have to meet at the library. I dread the thought. Shot or no shot, maybe I'll get lucky and catch the chicken pox between now and then.

Libby runs into the house first. "Tiny! We're home!" she sings out.

"He's not a dog," I say, hanging up my backpack. But just as the words are out of my mouth, the rabbit comes hopping down the hallway, his giant ears pricked forward, eager to see us.

"Tiny!" Libby cries at the same time I choke out, "What is that rabbit doing out of the closet?"

The rabbit slides to a stop on the smooth tile floor and wiggles his nose at us. Then he turns and runs back down the hall and into the kitchen.

How many puddles of pee will I have to clean up today? And how many of them are on my bed?

I run down the hall after the rabbit, Libby close behind me. We find him crouching under the kitchen table.

"All right, rabbit, come on out."

The rabbit wiggles its nose at me, but doesn't move.

"Grab some lettuce, Libby."

She does, and soon enough the rabbit is lured out from under the table. I grab him before he can run away again. "Take a look around and see if he's chewed on anything," I tell Libby. "Or peed on anything." Then I carry the rabbit up to my room.

The baby gate is locked in place in the door jamb. There's no sign of how he might have escaped. He couldn't have jumped out, could he?

Just as I expected, there's a puddle of pee on my bed. But there's no other clue how the rabbit got out. I dump the rabbit in the closet and start stripping my sheets.

I toss the bundle of bedding down the stairs, and then I go from room to room, looking for chewed furniture, carpeting, wires, clothes, or anything else the little monster has got his teeth into. But it doesn't seem like the rabbit has gone in any of the other bedrooms.

"Drew! Drew!"

Oh great. Looks like Libby's found something. I hurry downstairs and find her still in the kitchen.

"I think Tiny was hungry," she says, pointing to the pantry.

Bracing myself for the worst, I swing wide the pantry door. The floor is covered in flour, rice, oats, Cheerios and Frosted Flakes. Little rabbit footprints are smudged into the mess.

I groan. Loud.

It takes Libby and me just about an hour to clean it all up. We throw out as much of it as we can, but we can't throw out everything. I can just imagine trying to explain to Mom what happened to a ten-pound bag of flour and a five-pound bag of oats.

"Wait! I have an idea," Libby says. "Turn the bags around so the chewed parts are at the back."

"Libby, have you ever thought about a career in astrophysics?" I didn't plan on saying it. It just came out.

"Astro what?"

"Um, never mind." I'd rather swim through shark-infested water than explain to my sister that astrophysicists are really smart.

When we're finished, we stand back and admire our handiwork. It's like something with teeth was never in there.

The next morning is Saturday. But that doesn't stop Libby from waking me up at six in the morning.

"You do know what day it is, right?" I growl at her.

"I know," she says, "but Tiny needs his breakfast."

"Wonderful." I roll onto my back. "Why don't you clean his litter box while you're at it?"

"It's your turn," Libby says.

"No, it's not."

"Yes, it is! I did it last time." Libby crosses her arms.

"Well, I think it's your turn."

"I'll tell Mom and Dad if you don't."

"And then they'll take Tiny to the animal shelter."

That shuts her up.

"Okay, fine," Libby says. "But it's your turn next time."

"Fine by me." I tug my pillow over my head and go back to sleep.

A few hours later, the phone rings. Mom pokes her head into my room and tosses the phone onto my bed. "It's a girl."

What? Huh? Why are girls calling me?

I take the phone.

"Hi, this is Tabitha Schaeffer."

"Oh," I croak. "Hi Tabitha."

"So are we going to meet at the library after lunch or what?"

I actually don't want to meet at the library *ever*. But I haven't got much choice. "Um, I've got to clean my room. Remember?"

"Well, why don't you clean your room now?"

But that would mean getting out of bed.

"So? What do you say? I can be there at one o'clock."

"Yeah, okay, one o'clock."

"Okay, see you then," she says. Is that laughter or static I hear as she hangs up the phone?

Mom's eyebrows are raised.

"We have a science project."

"Oh?"

"Yeah, and she wants to work on it at the library."

"Well, all right," Mom says. "Just make sure your room is clean first."

"I will."

Mom leaves the doorway. I stare at the mess. At the clothes and papers and stuff piled high on my desk and dresser tops. At the lonely sock hanging from the light shade on my bed stand. Ugh. That stupid rabbit. I admit the first adjective to describe me wouldn't be "tidy," but since that rabbit showed up, my room's been bordering on a state of emergency.

I drag myself out of bed, find some clothes, and get dressed. I spend a few minutes debating whether or not to just push the mess under my bed. But Mom would never let me get away with that. I wish I could just shove all the mess into my closet like I would've done a week ago, but now the rabbit has taken over the closet. He's standing on his hind legs with his nose pressed against the mesh on the baby gate, giving me his most pathetic look. I throw a balled-up sock at him and he ducks and hops into his litter box, looking displeased.

Then I smell bacon frying. Maybe room cleaning can wait till after some breakfast.

I head downstairs to the kitchen. Libby is sitting at the counter, watching Dad poking thick bacon strips in a frying pan on the stove.

"Hey, kiddo," Dad says. "How about some breakfast?"

"Daddy's going to make pancakes!" Libby grins.

"Sounds good." I open the fridge and pull out the jug of orange juice. "I'm hungry."

Dad takes a card from Mom's recipe box. "Let's see. We'll need milk, eggs, flour . . ."

Libby's eyes lock with mine.

"Um, Dad," I say, "y'know, just bacon and eggs would be great. No need to go to all the trouble of making pancakes."

Dad frowns. "What? Suddenly you don't like my pancakes?"

"No . . . just . . ." I stammer.

"I think you make the best pancakes, Daddy!" Libby chimes in.

I give Libby a dirty look. "Maybe I changed my mind. Maybe I feel like just bacon and eggs today."

"Well, the rest of us want pancakes," Dad says, opening the pantry and pulling out the bag of flour.

Oh no!

A long stream of white powder pours out of the chewed-off corner of the flour bag. "What the—?" Dad says, when he sees the white trail on the floor. He holds the bag up, his eyes growing wide at the gaping hole. Then he starts pulling other bags from the pantry. Rice. Oats. Cornmeal. "Jess!" he shouts.

Mom's voice comes from upstairs. "Yeah?"

"I think you better get down here!"

Mom thumps down the stairs and rushes into the kitchen, breathless. "What? What is it? Are the kids okay?"

Dad holds up the leaking bags. "I think we've got rats."

"Rats?" Mom says, and then gasps. "The thumping!"

"That's what I was thinking, too." Dad nods. "I'll get some traps." And he heads out to the backyard.

"Are we still having pancakes?" Libby asks hopefully.

14
Like Taking off a Band-Aid

Possible Pets

Dog – Dad says I won't walk it
Cat – Mom is allergic
Ferret – Dad says they stink
Budgie – Mom says they're too loud and messy
Hamster – girl's pet
Guinea Pig – same as above
Hedgehog – Dad says they cost too much
Frog – Mom thinks it will get out
Gecko – same as above
Tarantula – Mom is terrified of spiders
Goldfish – dumb
Ant farm – Dad doesn't want pests in the house
Rabbit – boring
Pet rock – same as above

I smile to myself as I read over the list. I think I wrote it when I was eight or nine and was on my last campaign to get Mom and Dad to get me a pet. I'd totally forgotten about it until just now when I found it in my desk. Nope, rabbits are definitely not boring. But I'd rather lick sandpaper than have one now.

"Much better!" Mom says from the doorway of my bedroom.

I crumple up the list and toss it in the garbage, stuff the last dirty sock into the hamper, and take a look around my room. My desk and dresser tops are cleared. The shredded comic books are in the recycling. My bed is made. And the dirty laundry has been picked up. For a finishing touch, I spray some air freshener into the air.

"Libby and I are just heading to the grocery store. Do you want a ride to the library?"

I glance at the clock. It's already 12:45. Not that I want to go work on my project with Tabitha. But maybe I just need to do it and get it over with, like taking off a Band-Aid.

"Yeah, okay."

On the way to the library, Libby is still complaining that we didn't get pancakes for breakfast.

"That's why we're going to the store," Mom says. "To buy more flour and oats and rice and whatever else the rats got into. Then maybe we can make pancakes for dinner."

That seems to make her happy and she shuts up.

A few minutes later, we pull into the parking lot of the Douglas Bay branch of the Vancouver Island Regional Library and I climb out. "Call me when you're ready to be picked up." Mom has a twinkle in her eye I don't like. "Have fun!"

"We're just partners," I grumble.

"Oh, I know." Mom grins at me and pulls the car away from the curb.

Between the parking lot and the library entrance there is a sunken courtyard with benches for library-goers to sit and read, large, concrete planters full of flowers, and a few trees for shade. It's also where skateboarders like to hang out. Derek and Tanner are there, practicing their ollies and grinds.

"Hey, Drew!" Derek yells. "Where's your skateboard?"

I hitch my backpack higher on my shoulder. "I, uh, gotta work on my project."

"With your *girlfriend*?" Tanner laughs.

Derek makes kissing noises.

I open my mouth to tell them—again—that Tabitha is not my girlfriend but instead I say, "You know what? You guys sound jealous. Maybe you wish Tabitha was *your* girlfriend?"

"Gross!" Derek says.

"Yeah, no thanks!" Tanner makes gagging noises.

"You can keep her, Drew!"

Derek and Tanner double over laughing.

Just then a car pulls up and Tabitha gets out.

"Hi, Drew."

"Oh, uh, hey, Tabitha."

From behind us, Derek and Tanner are making loud kissing noises and howling with laughter.

My face burns.

Tabitha rolls her eyes. "Those guys are so immature. Just ignore them."

We start walking towards the library.

"Hey, what's that sound?" Tanner calls after us. "Are those *wedding* bells?"

"Mr. and Mrs. Montgomery," Derek hollers.

Tabitha whirls around. "Derek Redmond! You think you're so funny! Well, let's see who's laughing when I tell everyone at school you pick your nose and eat it too!"

"What? I don't—! You can't—" Derek sputters. Then he turns and takes off on his skateboard. For a second, Tanner stands there looking stunned, and then he turns and follows after Derek.

"Drew, you should close your mouth." Tabitha says. "You're catching flies."

I clamp my lips shut and follow her through the courtyard towards the library's entrance. We're about halfway there, when, without warning, Maya and Ally jump out from behind one of the planters, shrieking like a pair of rabid hyenas, and start spraying us with hot pink hair spray and purple Silly String. I'm so surprised, I scream. Yes, embarrassing as it is to admit, I, Drew Montgomery, scream like a little girl and start running for the library doors, Ally and her spray can hot on my heels.

Behind me, I can hear Tabitha yelling and then Maya screams. I glance behind me to see Tabitha with the can of Silly String, chasing Maya right out of the courtyard.

Ally sees it too and she turns and charges after Tabitha and Maya, screeching at the top of her lungs. It only takes a second for Tabitha to disarm Ally too, and then she's running out of the courtyard behind Maya, being chased by Tabitha until the cans run out and she lets the attackers go.

She jogs back to me, a huge grin on her face. Her hair and face are streaked with pink. Long purple streamers of Silly String hang from her clothes, dragging behind her on the concrete.

"Wow!" I whisper. "That was awesome."

Tabitha shrugs, picking Silly String from her hair. "I hate those two."

"So, uh, you still want to work on our project?"

She blinks. "Why wouldn't I?"

"Oh, I dunno." I wad up a bunch of Silly String and

throw it into a garbage can at the library entrance. "Maybe because we both look like we've been hit by a bad case of Halloween six months early?"

Tabitha laughs. "Yeah, I guess it wouldn't hurt to clean up a bit first. Pink isn't your best colour."

My ears burn.

We get a few strange looks when we walk into the library and make a beeline for the washrooms. It's as bad as I'd feared. My hair is pink. My face is pink. My clothes are even pink. I still have bits of Silly String stuck to me.

I do my best to wash off the pink, turn my hoodie inside out—whoever dreamed up reversible hoodies is a genius—and then I go find Tabitha, locate an empty table, and get to work.

For a while all we talk about is the project, looking up information on the Internet and in the books and encyclopedias in the library. We're getting a lot done and I'm starting to think having Tabitha for a partner isn't such a bad thing, when Tabitha says, "Um, Drew, there's a reason I wanted to be your partner for this project."

My heart starts pounding. Please don't let her ask to be my girlfriend! Please don't let her ask to be my girlfriend!

She leans across the table and says in a low whisper, "I know about your rabbit."

I blink. "My what?"

"You know, the rabbit you and your sister found."

I'm not sure whether to be relieved or angry. "How did—?"

"Your little sister told me. I saw her carrying that big book about rabbits to the bus stop and I asked her if she owned a rabbit. She told me everything."

Libby! When I get home . . . Oh, she is going to pay—big time.

"I thought maybe I could help you out," Tabitha continues. "I love rabbits."

Did I just hear that right? I could jump on the table and do a happy dance. My butt is so saved. "So you want to take him?"

She laughs. "What? No! I've already got two bunnies. I just thought I could help you with feeding him and stuff."

🥕   🥕   🥕

When Mom picks me up from the library an hour later, my head is spinning. And not just from all the information I've been reading for our project.

"So?" Mom says as I climb into the car. "How'd it go?"

"Good." I duck my head as I put my seatbelt on. I don't really want to talk about it.

"Wait, what's that in your hair?"

"What?" I pull down the visor and check the mirror. There's a patch of pink right above my left ear that I must've missed in the bathroom. "I, um . . ." My mind races to come up with an answer. I can't tell her the truth. And least not the whole truth. It's just too humiliating. "It's, uh, hairspray. Tabitha's hairspray. I, uh, didn't know it was pink."

Mom's eyebrows are raised, but she doesn't ask me about it anymore. "Better than lipstick, I suppose," she says.

And then I really do turn pink.

In the back seat, Libby is clutching a shopping bag like it holds some long lost treasure.

"What's in there?" I ask.

She grins and shows me a package of rabbit pellets and a pale-blue harness and leash.

"How did you get those?"

"Mom bought them for me. They're for Tiny Junior!" And she grins at me like we've just shared the greatest joke in the whole world.

I'm beginning to feel like the joke's on me.

15

Into the Woods

When we get back from the library, I go straight upstairs to shower and change. As I come out of the bathroom, Mom calls me into her bedroom. "Can I talk to you for a second?"

My heart thumps. What could she want to talk to me about? Has she found the rabbit? Or—*gulp*—my bike?

"Come sit down, sweetie." She pats the bed beside her.

I swallow, but do as she asks.

"Drew," she says. "I know this may be hard to talk about, but you know I've noticed you washing your sheets every day. I just want you to know I understand. It happens to a lot of people. But it's nothing to be embarrassed about. It used to happen to your Uncle Shawn."

Huh?

Then Mom reaches over and picks up a large blue plastic package from the other side of the bed and it all becomes clear. GoodNites underwear. My face burns so hot I think my skin might melt.

"Mom . . ." I say, but she cuts me off.

"I'm not disappointed or upset with you. This is just something that happens sometimes. But I am worried about you. Is there something at school that's upsetting you? Is taking care of Libby getting to be too much for you? Are you feeling stressed?"

"Mom! I'm *not* wetting the bed! It's the—" I stop myself just before I blurt out the truth. "I've just been, um, sweating a lot at night. That's all."

Mom doesn't look like she believes a word out of my mouth. "It's okay if you want to try to handle it on your own. I get that. I just want you to know that I'm here if you ever need me to help."

"I'm not wetting the bed, Mom! I'm not!"

"Maybe you could just give these a try?" She passes me the package of GoodNites. I don't want to touch it, let alone take it. For a moment the giant blue package hangs between us. "Please?"

The package crinkles as I grip it with fingers that no longer feel like they're attached to my hand.

Mom leans over and gives me a hug. "If you ever want to talk to me about it, you just have to say so. Okay?"

I leave my parents' bedroom on numb legs. I just hope Libby doesn't spot me with this enormous blue whale of a package. Wouldn't I just love *this* getting blabbed on the school bus on Monday.

Quick as I can I run into my room, determined to hide the GoodNites where no one will ever find them. I glance around for a good hiding spot, but the first thing I notice is the puddle of pee on my comforter. Not again! *Now* how did he get out? And worse yet, where is he? And what has he chewed on?

I stuff the package of GoodNites into a dresser drawer, then get down on all fours and look under the bed. A furry little nose pokes out from the darkness and wiggles at me.

"Get out of there!" I grab for the rabbit.

He ducks back under the bed and retreats into the darkness.

I grab my flashlight from my bed stand drawer and shine it under the bed. The rabbit is crouched in the farthest corner. Lying in front of him is my iPod—my "Mom and Dad are gonna kill me if anything bad happens to it" iPod—and about a dozen pieces of what used to be the cord to my earbuds.

"That's it, you stupid waste of oxygen! I don't care what it takes!" I spit through clenched teeth. "You are gone! Out of here! History!"

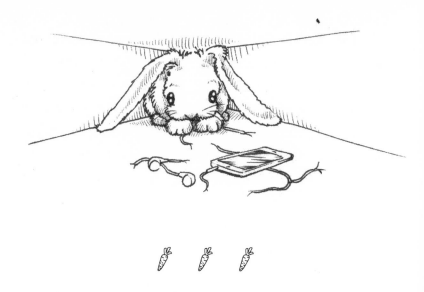

🥕   🥕   🥕

That night, as I lie in bed, staring at the weird shadows created on my ceiling by Libby's unicorn nightlight, all I can think about is the rabbit and my iPod. Sure it still works and I can buy new earbuds, but it's like the rabbit has it in for me and everything I own. Nothing is safe so long as that rabbit is in my bedroom.

In the closet, the rabbit is munching on his new pellets. From time to time, he hops in and out of his litter box, the newspaper crinkling under his feet. Help or no help from Tabitha, I want him gone. But I can't do it, as long as Libby keeps holding my bike over my head.

Then it hits me: What I have to do is get rid of my bike. If the bike is really and truly gone, Libby can't prove I ever took it into the woods. She can't prove I broke it. She can't prove it wasn't stolen. If she tried to tell Mom and Dad, I'd tell them she was lying. I'd tell her to prove it. And when she couldn't, I'd be free.

So, the next day, after lunch, I march up the road, past the ditch where we found the rabbit, past the school bus stop, around the bend in the road, and then jump another ditch, and follow the narrow dirt trail into the woods.

When I get to the stump, I squeeze through the gap in the side. In the dim light I can just make out the spot where I'd hidden my bike. There's a dent in the ground where it used to be, but my bike is gone!

Oh no! Oh no! Oh no!

I fall to my knees and start digging through the leaves and pine needles covering the ground, but there's nothing there. No clue where it's gone.

Who could've found it? The police? My heart hammers against my chest. If they've found it, I'm so dead. Dad will find out I took it into the woods and broke it. I'll be grounded forever. I'm pacing up and down inside the old stump. But they would've called when they found it, wouldn't they? Of course they would. So who else could it be? The homeless guys? What would they want with a broken kids' bike? No, couldn't be them. Was it Libby? I do a mental rewind on the last week, but I can't think of a single time when I didn't know where she was. She's been too busy with the rabbit. Still, it had to be her. Who else could it be? No one else knew it was here.

I race home to find out what she knows.

When I get home, Libby is having another tea par-ty—in my bedroom. Tiny Junior is sitting in one chair, wearing a pink satin dress and bonnet, with a bowl of rabbit pellets and carrots in front of him. The real Tiny is sitting in another chair, wearing that stupid purple cape again, with his paws on the table, his nose stuck in his own bowl of rabbit pellets.

"Libby! What are you *doing*?"

"Can't you see? We're having a tea party," she says and sips daintily from an empty teacup, her little finger extended.

"I mean what are you doing in my *bedroom*?"

"Well, you said Tiny had to stay in your room."

I groan. "Where's Mom?"

"She's gone to the hairdresser."

"And Dad?"

"He's in his office."

"Libby—I just—I think the rabbit needs to stay in the closet on the weekends. What if Dad came upstairs right now?"

Libby looks heartbroken. "But you never let me play with Tiny. He always has to stay in your room. It's not fair!" A big, fat tear slides down her face, then another, and then the dam breaks. "You're not fair! I hate you!"

And she gets up and runs into her bedroom and slams the door.

The rabbit is staring at me.

"What? This is all your fault anyway."

He wiggles his tail at me, and then hops onto the table and starts eating the rabbit pellets out of Tiny Junior's bowl.

"Hey! What's with all the slamming doors?" Dad calls from downstairs.

"Nothing!" I call back.

"Well, I'm trying to work here."

"Sorry!"

I sit down on my bed. Now I've done it. I need to find out what Libby knows about my bike, but instead I've sent her crying to her room. I sigh.

"C'mon, rabbit. Let's go cheer Libby up." I pick up the rabbit, who looks rather displeased to be torn away from his bowl of pellets, and go knock on Libby's door.

"Go away!"

"Libby, I'm sorry. Can I come in?"

"No!"

"I brought Tiny." I open the door a crack and hold the rabbit up for her to see.

"Tiny can stay, but you can't." She's sitting on her bed, her arms wrapped around her knees.

I want to say, "Fine!" and dump the rabbit and stomp out of the room. But I need to find out what happened to my bike, so I gently set the rabbit on her bed and stroke his ears. He lays his head on the mattress, closes his eyes, and chatters his teeth. I've never heard that sound before.

"Aw! Look!" Libby squeals. "He's tooth-purring."

"Tooth-what?"

"Tooth-purring. It's in the book." Libby grabs the

book from her bed stand and flips through until she finds the page she's looking for. "See, it says rabbits grind their teeth when they're happy, just like cats purring. It's called tooth-purring."

"Uh, yeah, real fascinating."

"Are you a happy bunny?" Libby coos at the rabbit. He pricks an ear at her.

"Anyway, I wanted to ask you something, Libby."

"What?"

"Well, I was just wondering if you've gone up to the woods lately."

"No." She frowns. "Why would I?"

"Oh, I dunno."

"Drew, you're being weird."

"Then you haven't seen my bike?"

"You mean your *broken* bike?"

I roll my eyes. "Yes, my broken bike."

"Not since you broke it."

"So you haven't gone up into the woods or seen my bike?"

"*No!*"

"Okay, that's all I wanted to know."

I get up and leave Libby's room. In the hallway I let go with a major victory dance. I'm free! Finally free. It's time for little bunny to go.

16
"Goodbye, Rabbit."

Monday morning, after Libby and I take our seats on the bus, Tabitha slides into the seat behind us.

"How's your bunny?" she says.

"Oh, he's great!" Libby says. "I got him his own harness and leash so we can take him for walks now."

"I bet he'll like that." Tabitha smiles. "Lolly and Oscar like to take walks too. Well, Lolly more so than Oscar. He just likes to lie around and eat."

Libby giggles.

The whole way to school Libby and Tabitha talk about rabbits. I wish I had my iPod so I could crank up the volume and drown them out, but until I can go buy some new earbuds without Mom and Dad finding out, it's stuck at home in the drawer of my night stand. Fortunately, I don't think the rabbit has learned to open drawers yet.

"So, Drew," Tabitha says. "When did you want to get together again to work on our project?"

Even though I know Tabitha doesn't want to be my girlfriend, the words "get together" still make me feel queasy. "Uh, whenever. I guess."

"Okay, how about tomorrow after school?"

"Um, yeah, sure."

The bus pulls up to the school and we all climb off.

"Did you hear, Drew?" Libby says. "Lolly and Oscar like to sit on the couch with Tabitha. I want Tiny to sit on the couch with us, too."

"Yeah, Libby. Sounds great."

"And Lolly and Oscar are bonded too—that means they're like married. Aw! Isn't that so cute?"

"Real cute, Libby."

"I think we should get a girl bunny for Tiny."

"Yeah—*what*? Have you forgotten? We aren't even supposed to have one rabbit."

Libby looks disappointed as she shuffles off to line up with the other grade two kids.

Quentin is already standing in the lineup outside our classroom. He has a few scabbed-over pockmarks on his face and about the same amount on each arm. I'm so relieved to see him, it takes every bit of self-control I've got not to throw my arms around him.

"You're back!" I say. "I've missed you so much."

Quentin laughs. "Whoa! Dude. Calm down. It was only six days."

"You have *no* idea how long six days can be. Promise me you won't get chicken pox ever again."

Quentin laughs again. "I don't think you can catch chicken pox twice. But I'll try."

The bell rings and we file into the school.

For the first time in a week, the morning flies by. If Maya and Ally were ignoring me on Friday, I don't even exist to them today. No smirks, no giggles, no glances in my direction. The only hint I get that anything happened at all at the library on Saturday is when I happen to catch Maya blushing a bit when Tabitha walks past her desk. But otherwise, things seem to be back to normal. Soon it's recess and Quentin and I hurry out to our corner of the playing field where we can talk about everything that's happened the last week.

The first thing I do is tell him about the rabbit. About how we found it and how Libby blackmailed me into keeping it and how it's peed on my bed every single day, and kept escaping, and made a meal of everything else.

"That's really lame," Quentin says when I'm done. "So what are you going to do about it?"

"Get rid of it, is what. Just as soon as I get the chance." I kick a dandelion puff and it explodes into hundreds of tiny seeds. "You don't know anybody who wants a rabbit, do you?"

"Sorry, can't help you there."

"Stupid animal." I kick another dandelion, and then another. "Why do I have to get stuck with the dumbest animal on the planet?"

"Dumber even than a slug?" Quentin makes a face that I guess is supposed to look like a slug.

"Pretty darn close!" I wind up and kick another dandelion. This one still has the flower on it and the yellow head goes flying right over the fence.

Quentin laughs and soon we're both kicking dandelion tops over the fence into the yard on the other side. At least until the old lady that lives there spots us and hobbles outside onto her patio to yell at us about it.

Quentin and I take off running across the field.

Breathless, we flop down in the courtyard outside the gym. "So what was it like having the chicken pox?" I ask when I've caught my breath again.

"It wasn't so bad," Quentin says. "Except for the itching. I sometimes felt like scratching my skin off. But I got to stay in bed most of the day. And Mom rented me a bunch of video games and movies so I wasn't totally bored."

Now I wish my mom hadn't got me the shots and I'd got the chicken pox instead of Quentin. Video games and movies? Lying in bed all day? Sounds way better than the week I'd just had.

Quentin must have picked up my train of thought,

because he leans over and whispers, "I heard what Maya and Ally did at the library."

I groan. "Don't remind me."

"You want to get even?"

"Do I ever."

"Well, then we need to make a plan."

For a minute we both sit thinking, munching on our recess snacks.

"I know!" I say. "We get some fish—"

"Anchovies!" Quentin's eyes sparkle.

"Yeah, anchovies, and we put them in their desks—"

"Wait a second. And they're not going to notice that the second they walk into class?"

He has a point. "Okay, then, how about this? We'll get some poison ivy and stick it in their gym bags."

"Where are we going to get poison ivy? I don't even think it grows around here."

"Wait! I've got it. How about we take the *anchovies* and stick *them* in their gym bags."

"Drew! That's awesome!" Quentin is grinning from ear to ear. "They're gonna die of embarrassment."

"Can you just see their faces when they have to walk out of the change room smelling like fish? And Mr. Murray says our gym strip stinks."

Quentin and I burst out laughing.

For the rest of the day, neither of us can even look at Maya or Ally without struggling not to laugh out loud.

It's probably a good thing they're doing such a good job ignoring us, or they'd figure something was up.

🥕 🥕 🥕

After school, there's a message in the office for me from Mom. Libby is going over to a friend's house after school and I won't need to babysit her. This is my chance!

I can't board the bus fast enough. I find a seat and slide into it. Everyone else is laughing and talking and taking their time choosing seats. I want to jump up and yell at them to hurry it up. This is a matter of life and death.

Toby Neville plunks down on the bench beside me. I don't think I've said more than five words to Toby all year. He spends all his spare time in the computer lab or the library. And we haven't been partnered up for any projects.

"Hi, Drew."

"Uh, hey, Toby."

For a while, Toby just sits there and fiddles with the zipper on his backpack.

Once again, I wish I had my iPod.

"I have something to tell you," Toby says at last, peering at me through his thick glasses.

"Oh?"

He glances back down at his backpack. "Yeah, uh, I heard about what happened at the library on Saturday."

Is there anyone who *hasn't*?

"I, um, feel really bad about that." More fiddling with the zipper. "See, I'm the one that wrote on the whiteboard."

I feel like somebody just dumped a bucket of freezing cold water over my head. Did I just hear that right? My eyes must be bugging out of my head.

Toby drops his gaze. "Yeah, so, I'm, um, sorry."

All I can do is stare at him. "But—but—why?"

Toby's face turns bright red. The dopey grin on his face tells me everything. I can almost see the cartoon hearts in his eyes.

I shake my head. "Which one?"

"Maya," he says, breathlessly.

Yuck.

At last, the bus pulls up to my stop and I squeeze past him and push my way off the bus.

As fast as I can, I run up the road and into the house, dropping my coat and backpack in the hallway. Then I grab the phone book in the kitchen, look up the listing for the Arbutus Animal Shelter, and dial the number.

After three rings, a woman answers.

"Hi," I say, "I have a rabbit that needs to find a new home."

"I'm sorry, our small animal room is currently full. Can I take your name and we'll put your pet on our waiting list?"

"Well, he's not really our pet. We found him in a box on the road."

"Oh, he's a stray, is he? Is there any way your family can keep him till space becomes available? We simply haven't got the room right now."

I can't believe what I'm hearing. This is my only chance to get rid of the rabbit. "No! The rabbit has to go now!"

"Excuse me?" the woman says, her voice rising in pitch.

"You have to understand. He eats everything in sight. He's ruining my life!"

"Is this a prank?"

"No! No, it's not a prank!"

"Well, it sure sounds like a prank, and I don't think it's very funny. I'm hanging up the phone now."

"No! No you—!"

CLICK!

I stare at the dead phone. Now what do I do? Do I make up a bunch of "Free to Good Home" signs and hang them in the neighbourhood? Do I go house to house and ask if anyone wants a rabbit? I don't have that kind of time. The rabbit has to go *now*.

I get up and pace the floor. There's got to be something—wait! What if he accidentally got outside? And what if the back gate happened to be open? And what if he just wandered off?

I run upstairs and burst through the door into my room. "Oh, rabbit, I've got a surprise for you." The rabbit is not in my closet. Instead, he's curled up, asleep on my bed. Beside him is a puddle of pee. I want to scream. Not again!

He yawns and stretches when he sees me and hops over to the edge of the bed, wiggling his nose at me.

"All right, rabbit, this is both our lucky day. You're going free."

I scoop him up, carry him downstairs, and drop him in the backyard. For good measure, I prop open the back gate with a brick from behind the tool shed.

"Goodbye, rabbit," I say.

Then I go back inside and shut the door, leaving the rabbit in the backyard, gobbling up grass like he hasn't eaten in a week.

I'm stretched out on the couch playing video games and gorging myself on dill pickle chips, celebrating my newfound freedom, when I hear an all-too-familiar *THUMP!* from the back porch.

It can't be! I glance down the hall to the back door. The rabbit is standing on his back legs, his front paws pressed against the glass, giving me his "how can you resist such a cute rabbit as me?" face. Unbelievable!

At first, I decide to ignore him. Maybe if I don't open the door, the stupid animal will realize he's not wanted and go away.

THUMP!

I can't hear you rabbit. La la la.

THUMP!

Not working. Nobody here.

THUMP!

Why won't he just leave? I glance at the clock. It's

way too close to five o'clock. Mom and Dad could be here any minute. I can't risk them finding the rabbit on the back porch.

I get up and open the door. The rabbit is sitting on the doormat, like a dog waiting to be let in.

"Shoo! Go away! Don't you understand what it means to be free?"

But the rabbit just sits there, looking at me and wiggling its nose.

"Hyah! Get lost!" I yell and flap my arms.

The rabbit crouches low, looking like he's about to turn and run, but he doesn't move.

"Please! Just *go*!"

But he won't.

I have no other choice but to let him back into the house. He immediately hops upstairs to my room and jumps into his litter box.

I groan. Loud.

It's just like that old Fred Penner song. Except, instead of the cat came back, the rabbit did.

17
Help!

After dinner, the phone rings.

"It's Quentin!" Mom yells up the stairs.

I drop the picture I'm drawing of Maya and Ally prancing around with fish heads sticking out of their clothes onto my bed and hurry to answer it.

"We've got a problem," Quentin says. "No anchovies."

"Oh, man!" I slump down on the floor. "We don't have any either. Not even any sardines."

"We've got a can of tuna. Do you think that would work?"

"I guess. Fish is fish. Just don't forget the can opener!"

After I hang up, I head back into my room to finish my drawing. But there's the rabbit, sitting on my bed again, chewing my picture to shreds. At least this time there's no puddle of pee.

As if reading my mind, the rabbit lifts its tail and relieves itself on my comforter. Then it hops down and scoots under the bed.

Why me?

With the help of my hockey stick, I persuade the rabbit out from underneath my bed and back into the closet. He hops into his litter box and glares at me.

I glare right back. Then I notice something. I call Libby.

She comes into the room with her toothbrush stuck in her mouth. "What?"

"Does the rabbit look bigger to you?"

She peers over the baby gate. "I guess. A little."

"No really. Does the rabbit look bigger or not?"

Libby shrugs. "Maybe a tiny bit bigger."

I shake my head. "Must be my imagination."

She leaves the room to finish brushing her teeth.

But I don't think I'm imagining things. Before, when the rabbit sat in the litter box, he seemed so small, like a kid in an Olympic-sized swimming pool. But now he looks more like a kid in a kiddie pool. Not quite so little anymore.

🥕 🥕 🥕

When I wake up the next morning, the rabbit is curled up at my feet. From under the covers, I give him a boot. He jumps off the bed and sits on the floor blinking and looking displeased.

"No way am I changing my sheets *again*! Go use your litter box."

He blinks at me, and then hops off to the closet. The gate is up, blocking his way back inside, but that doesn't even faze him. He takes an enormous leap that lands him partway over the top, then he pulls himself up the rest of the way, until he's perched on top of the gate like a long-eared, roosting chicken. And then, ever so gracefully, he drops down into the closet.

Unbelievable.

Libby comes sneaking into my room then, lettuce in hand, to feed the rabbit.

"Did you just see that?" I say.

"What?"

"The rabbit! He just jumped over the baby gate."

Libby's eyes grow big. "Oh, wow! So that's how he got out."

"I guess we're just going to have to keep the closet door closed every day."

"But, Drew—!"

"No way! He's already eaten my gym strip, my comic books, my computer, and my iPod. Next he'll be eating the furniture."

I swing my legs out of bed. Just as I do, my bed teeters and collapses to the floor. *CRRAASSH!*

Libby and I just stare at each other.

At that moment, Mom and Dad both appear in the doorway. Mom's still in her bathrobe. Dad's shirt is unbuttoned, his tie dangling from his neck.

"What was *that*?"

"What's going on in here?"

I notice Libby quietly pushing the closet door closed behind her.

"I—I—don't know!" I stammer.

Dad drops to his knees and looks under the bed. "Good lord! Look at this, Jess!"

Mom kneels down and takes a look. "Well, I—what on earth could have chewed through the legs like that?"

Mom and Dad exchange confused glances.

I climb out of bed to take a look myself. The legs of my bed look like they've been gnawed by little beavers.

"Wow!" I say. "We must be dealing with super rats!"

Mom goes pale and glances at Dad. "You think it was rats, Todd?"

"I don't know. Something with teeth got under there. I'm calling the exterminator," Dad says.

Exterminator? Oh no!

While Dad goes downstairs to make the call, Mom heads back into her bedroom to get dressed. "Hurry up, you two, it's time to get ready for school."

She doesn't have to tell me twice. I throw on my clothes and race downstairs to the kitchen.

Dad's already talking on the phone when I get there. "Yes, yes. Okay, that's great. Yes, I'll be at the house then. Thanks for your time."

Dad hangs up. "Hey, Jess!" he yells.

"Yes?" Mom's voice comes from the stairwell.

"The exterminator's coming at eleven o'clock."

Eleven o'clock? Oh no!

Mom comes into the kitchen a moment later. She's got a brush in one hand and a jar of makeup in the other. "Eleven o'clock?"

"It's the only appointment they've got this week. I'll just have to take an early lunch."

I feel lightheaded. There's no way around it. The exterminator is going to find the rabbit.

Now I need help.

While Mom and Dad are talking in the kitchen, I run upstairs and grab the phone from their room and scroll through the Caller ID list for Tabitha's number. There's no number for Schaeffer, but there is one for Henderson. I almost drop the phone. That wasn't Tabitha that called Saturday morning. It was Ally! And no doubt Maya was there too. But then how did Tabitha know what time to meet at the library? They must have called her too. I bet they got Ally's brother to pretend to be me. I clench my fists. Now I can't *wait* to get them back. They are so going to pay.

The phone book is downstairs, but so are Dad and Mom. How am I going to make this call without them knowing?

Quietly, I creep downstairs and through the hall to the kitchen doorway. Dad has left for work and Mom's rushing around the kitchen looking for her keys. When her back is turned, I slink into the room, pull out the phone book from the drawer and then dash back to the hallway.

Too late.

"What are you doing with the phone book?" Mom calls after me.

I pull up short in the doorway. "I, um, have to call Tabitha about, um, about my project!"

Mom looks confused, but then says, "Oh, all right." And goes back to looking for her keys.

I dial Tabitha's number. Just as it starts ringing, I realize I'm going to sound like an idiot: *"My Mom and Dad think we have rats and they've called an exterminator and now I don't know what to do with the rabbit."*

But before I can hang up, a man answers.

"Oh, uh, hi, can I talk to Tabitha, please?"

"Sorry, she's already left for the bus. Can I take a message?"

"Uh, no, it's okay. I ride the same bus. I'll talk to her there."

I hang up the phone.

Now what?

I run upstairs. I'm not entirely sure what I'm going to do, but I need to get that rabbit out of my room before I have to leave for school. School! That's it! I scoop up the rabbit from the closet floor, where he's having a nap. Then I grab my backpack and lower the rabbit into it. His eyes bug out of his head and he starts scrabbling. I push him down. "Sorry, rabbit. You're just going to have to come to school with me."

Then I pour the pellets in his food bowl on top of him and zip the bag closed.

I quickly empty his litter box into my wastebasket and tie the bag closed. I'll take that to the garbage can on the way out the door to the bus. I remove the baby gate and dump it in the bottom of the closet. Then I pull half the clothes out of my dresser and throw them onto the floor of the closet, covering the bowl, dish, newspaper, litter box, Mr. Wuzzy, the baby gate, and everything else in there that belongs to the rabbit. I'm going to have a lot of laundry to do later, but better than getting caught with a rabbit in my closet.

"Come on, Drew. You're going to miss the bus!" Mom yells.

"Coming!" I grab my backpack and the bag of garbage and run downstairs.

On the bus, I wait for Libby to go sit with her friends,

then I slide into the seat beside Tabitha.

"Hi," she says, looking surprised.

"I need your help."

"Oh, and how are you doing today, too?"

"Sorry, I just don't know what else to do." I unzip my backpack and two caramel-coloured ears poke through the opening, followed by a very displeased face.

"Oh!" Tabitha says.

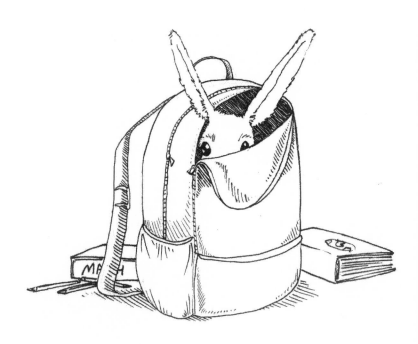

"Yeah." I push the rabbit back down and zip the bag closed. He wiggles and scrabbles for a moment before he settles down again.

"What are you going to do?" Tabitha says.

"I don't know. I was hoping you'd help me."

Tabitha stares at me. "How? What am I supposed to do?"

"I dunno. I thought you knew all about rabbits."

"Yeah, how to feed them, and trim their nails, and what to put in their litter box."

I don't know what to say to that. "*Please*, Tabitha. You *have* to help me!"

"Oh, all right. Give me a bit and I'll see what I can think of."

18
No Rabbit

The first thing Quentin does when I get to school is lean over and whisper: "The can opener is in my backpack." And he winks at me.

Of course, right at that moment, the last thing on my mind is getting revenge on Maya and Ally, so I just stare at him, not understanding.

"The can opener. You know. For the *tuna*." He says it really slow, looking at me like he's concerned I've completely lost it.

"Oh, *right*!" I force a smile onto my face, even though I'm not feeling like smiling at all. I'm too worried about what I'm going to do with the rabbit. He starts wiggling again. I hitch my backpack further up my shoulder and he stops.

"I can't wait for gym class!" Quentin rubs his hands

together like a villain in a cartoon movie.

And *I* can't wait to take this rabbit back home. Part of me wants to turn around right now and start hoofing it. It might take me all morning, but it would be better than trying to figure out what to do with a rabbit at school. Now I wish I'd chosen today to play sick.

But then the bell rings and I have no choice but to trudge into the school with the other kids.

While everyone else hurries to hang up their coats and bags, I carefully set my backpack on the floor and take my time changing into my inside shoes.

Quentin appears at my side. "Hey, c'mon, hurry up! The second bell is gonna go!"

Everyone has gone into class but Owen Abernethy, who's just showed up late.

"Quentin, we've got another problem." I unzip my backpack and the rabbit pokes his head up, his nose wiggling a mile a minute.

"What the heck?" Quentin's eyes widen.

"I didn't know what else to do! Mom and Dad called in an exterminator."

"So let the exterminator do his job!" Quentin says.

"Are you kidding? If my parents found out I was hiding a rabbit in my closet, I'd be grounded for life. No computer, no video games, no nothing!"

Quentin sucks in a breath.

The rabbit is struggling to get out of the backpack. Before he can wriggle free and take off down the hallway, I grab him and push him back down inside. Then, with one hand keeping the rabbit from hopping out, I pull out my homework with the other and zip it closed again. Leaving the backpack sitting on the floor, instead of hanging it on the hook, Quentin and I hurry into the classroom.

"I just hope he doesn't pee in there," I say.

No, he does one better. When we have to hand in our Math homework, I realize the rabbit has nibbled my worksheet down to nothing. Only two problems remain out of fifteen. I can't hand this in. I can't just say: "Sorry, Mr. Plonski. The rabbit ate my homework."

I sigh. "I think I forgot my homework at home," I tell him.

"You can hand it in tomorrow. But if you forget again, I'm going to have to mark you a zero."

I sigh again. "I know."

All through the rest of math class I can't stop thinking about the rabbit in my backpack. He's probably not only peed in there, but he's probably chewed the insides to shreds too. I'm just glad I wasn't dumb enough to leave any more homework in there.

Quentin, on the other hand, seems to be only thinking about our revenge plan. And on any other day, I'd be right there with him. When he catches my eye across the classroom, he plugs his nose and makes a gagging face. I pretend to laugh, but inwardly I groan. That's the face I'm most likely going to make when I open my backpack.

Finally, I can't stand it anymore. I put up my hand.

"Yes, Drew," says Mr. Plonski.

"May I use the washroom?"

"Can't it wait for recess?"

"No. I really have to go."

The class giggles.

"Very well. You have three minutes."

I nearly knock over my chair as I jump up and race out of the classroom.

The cloakroom is completely silent. No scratching or scrabbling sounds coming from my backpack. I hope I haven't suffocated the thing. Yes, I want to get rid of him. But I don't want to be responsible for murder, either.

I kneel down and, as quietly as possible, unzip my backpack.

The rabbit is lying in the bottom, looking like a little caramel-coloured marshmallow, fast asleep. He wiggles his nose at me, but doesn't move. With a sigh of relief, I close my backpack and head back to class.

I manage to check on the rabbit again during social studies class. I'm sure some of the kids must think I've got bladder problems, but I don't care. All I can think about is the rabbit. But he hasn't moved a whisker. For a moment I wonder if he's still alive. But he blinks in the sudden light, and his nose starts wiggling.

"Good rabbit," I say and zip closed my backpack.

By the time the recess bell rings, I've stopped worrying about the rabbit and am starting to get excited about getting revenge on Maya and Ally. Gym class is right after recess.

Tabitha comes over to my desk as I'm packing up my books.

"I have an idea," she says just as Quentin appears beside me. He gives Tabitha a weird look. Tabitha crosses her arms.

"Are you coming or what?" he says.

"She's helping me with my problem," I explain.

"Great! Go for it, Tabitha!" Quentin says. "Come on, Drew. We need to discuss, um, our, um, well, you know."

"Just a sec, Quentin." I turn to Tabitha. "What's your idea?"

Now Quentin crosses his arms.

"Well," she says. "You know how Ms. Worthington used to have Skittles, the guinea pig?"

Quentin laughs. "You mean the guinea pig that went home for the weekend with a kid with three cats?"

Tabitha gives Quentin a look that says if Mr. Plonski wasn't still in the room she'd thump him. "Yes, *that* guinea pig. Anyway, I think his old cage is in the storage room in the primary wing. It's a bit small for a rabbit, but Tiny should be safe in there till after school." She gives me a pleased grin.

"Much safer than in my backpack, anyway," I agree. "But isn't that room locked 24/7?"

"There are advantages to being on the Leadership Committee." Tabitha winks and holds up a key on a purple lanyard that says "Too Cool for School" in bright orange letters.

"Perfect!" I say and Tabitha and I head out of the classroom.

"But what about our, uh, discussion?" Quentin asks, following behind us.

"Don't worry, Quentin. We'll still have plenty of time for that!"

But when we get out to the cloakroom, it's obvious right away that something's wrong. My backpack is lying in the middle of the floor like a deflated balloon with a gaping hole in the side.

"Oh no!" says Tabitha.

I grab my backpack and hurriedly unzip it. There's a puddle of pee inside. No rabbit.

"That can't be good," Quentin says.

"We've got to find him!" I stand up, scanning the corridor, searching for any clue as to where the rabbit could've gone.

"I'll check the primary wing," Tabitha volunteers and hurries off in that direction.

"Quentin, you check the library and gym. I'll check around here."

"I'm on it!" Quentin says.

Just then, Mr. Plonski comes out into the hallway. "Outside, gentlemen," he says.

"But I, uh, I forgot something in the library," I say, edging in that direction.

"Nope," he says. "You can find it later. No unsupervised students in the school."

And just like that, Quentin and I find ourselves outside.

"What are we going to do?" I say, beginning to panic.

"Dude, don't worry," Quentin says. "Tabitha will find him. She sounds like a rabbit expert."

"She does know a lot about rabbits," I say.

"Of course she does. Don't worry about him. By the time recess is over, she'll most likely have him snug as a bug in that guinea pig cage."

We head out to the far corner of the playing field, flop down on the grass and go over the details of our revenge plan again.

"What if one of the girls comes while I'm in there?" I say.

Quentin's eyebrows come together as he thinks that one over. "Then I'll try to distract them. If I can't,

I'll knock three times. Then you can hide or, if worse comes to worst, run out on the fire escape."

"Okay. Good idea." I grin. "I can't wait to see their faces when they come out of the change room," I say.

"They'll have to wear their sweaty gym strip for the rest of the day!" Quentin says.

And we both burst out laughing again.

Then the bell rings and Quentin and I run back to the school.

Tabitha meets up with us at the door.

"Did you find him?" all three of us ask at the same time.

"Why not?" Quentin says.

"You didn't?" I say.

"Oh no!" Tabitha says.

19
THUNK!

There's no time to spend looking for the rabbit. Gym class is next and we only have time to grab our gym bags and run down to the gym to get changed. Mr. Murray makes the whole class do push-ups if anyone's late. Of course, that doesn't stop me from looking in every corner and glancing under every shelf and chair and table on the way there.

We quickly change. Then Quentin gives me a thumbs-up and we head out to line up alphabetically along the wall. After running laps around the gym for ten minutes, Mr. Murray sets up a game of kick ball. After a few innings, Quentin nods at me.

"May I use the washroom?" I ask.

There are a few giggles. I seriously am going to have a reputation for bladder problems after this. But seeing Maya and Ally humiliated after everything they've done to me this last week will be so worth it.

Mr. Murray nods. "Make it quick, Drew."

I trot off to the change rooms. First, I grab the tin of tuna and the can opener from Quentin's gym bag in the boys' change room. Then, when I'm sure nobody's looking, I push through the door into the girls' change room.

My heart is thudding against my chest. I've never been in the girls' change room before. I'm not sure what I'll find. I hope there isn't a bunch of girls' underwear hanging everywhere. But it's pretty much the same as the boys' room. Gym bags hang from rows of hooks along the walls, a few shirts or socks lay on the long metal benches underneath. On the left-hand wall, there are a few change stalls and the tiny closet that serves as a bathroom. Just everything is laid out exactly the opposite to the boys' room.

That and it doesn't smell as bad.

Right away I get to work, going from bag to bag until I find the pink and black designer bag that is Maya's. Ally's identical bag, of course, is hanging on the hook right next to it.

My hands tremble as I clip the can opener onto the side of the tin of tuna and start cranking. But for whatever reason, the blade on the can opener doesn't break the lid. I try again. And again it doesn't work. Unbelievable!

My heart is really hammering against my ribs now. My hands are shaking so hard I can barely hold the tin or the can opener as I attempt a third time to open the tuna. I really hope Quentin is outside standing guard.

Suddenly the door squeaks open behind me. I drop the can. It hits the side of the metal bench with a loud *CLANG!*

"What the heck are you doing?" Quentin calls in a hoarse whisper.

"The can! It won't open!"

"Oh, for—give it to me!"

I run over and hand him the tin and the can opener.

There's now a large dent in the top. He struggles for a bit, then finally the lid gives and he starts cranking open the tin. We both grin.

"All right, go for it!" Quentin hands me the tin and the can opener and disappears back outside.

For a moment I hesitate. Then I remember how embarrassing it was to walk into the library, sprayed head to toe with pink hairspray. I march over to the girls' gym bags and empty the can's contents into them.

Victorious, I toss the can into the garbage and run out of the girls' change room. "I did it! I did it!" But Quentin isn't standing outside the change room. Quentin is nowhere to be seen. Instead, Mrs. DiCastillo, the principal, is there.

"Did *what*?" she asks, her eyes narrowing. "And why were you in the girls' change room?"

"I, um, that was the girls' change room?" I say, trying to sound innocent.

"Do I look like I was born yesterday?" Mrs. DiCastillo crosses her arms. "I think perhaps we need to have a chat in my office."

"But—!" Oh no! I drop the can opener on the floor with a *THUNK!*

🥕 🥕 🥕

If you've never been sent to the principal's office, let me tell you, it's the worst feeling in the world. I imagine it has the same sense of doom as being sent to the electric chair or being forced to walk the plank.

It takes Mrs. DiCastillo all of two seconds to figure out what I've been doing in the girls' change room. All she has to do is push open the door and the strong smell of fish comes wafting out. In another two seconds she knows which gym bags—the dripping ones—have been my targets.

She carries the soggy bags into the gym and says, "Whose bags are these?"

Maya and Ally's eyebrows go up, followed by their hands.

"I'm sorry, girls. I'll call your parents to bring you

a change of clothes," Mrs. DiCastillo announces and turns on her heel, dragging me with her.

I can feel Maya and Ally's glares burning into my back as Mrs. DiCastillo marches me out of the gym and down the hall, past a group of gawking grade threes hanging artwork on the bulletin board outside their classroom. She directs me to a chair in her office. I swallow hard and sit down.

She places the can opener on the desk in front of her, pulls up her chair, and clasps her hands in front of her. "Now, please explain to me, Drew, why you think emptying a can of tuna into Maya and Ally's gym bags is acceptable?"

My hands are getting sweaty now and my heart is thudding. What is she going to do to me? I remember my grandpa telling me stories about kids getting the strap when he was in school. They don't still do that, do they? There isn't a leather belt hidden in the large wooden desk in front of me, is there? I stare at my lap.

"I must say, I'm *very* disappointed with your behaviour lately. We do not tolerate any form of bullying at this school."

"Bullying?" I say, before I can stop myself. "If you want to talk about bullying, talk to Maya and Ally!"

Mrs. DiCastillo considers this for a moment, then she leans back and crosses her arms. "Drew, I know the girls wrote an embarrassing message about you on the whiteboard. But I'd hardly call that bullying. You provoked them and they retaliated. And, might I add, they were disciplined for it. They both wrote you an apology letter and promised never to do anything like that at school again."

I flush hot, then cold. Suddenly it all makes sense. Why nothing happened on Friday, then the ambush at the library on Saturday. Those two made sure to get their revenge when no teachers or principals could get them into trouble.

"Your behaviour, on the other hand, has crossed the line." She stabs her desk with her forefinger as if to drive home her point. "Damaging other people's property is bordering on criminal. Are you ready to pay for the damages? Have you thought about that? I don't believe you have, or you would not have done this. And trying to humiliate them like you did is completely unacceptable!"

I slump down in my seat. This is so unfair. It should be Maya and Ally sitting in here getting read the riot act. Not me!

"I believe a phone call to your parents is in order. You may wait in the hallway."

My stomach drops onto the floor so hard, I think it leaves a dent.

20
Trouble!

I leave the office on legs as stiff as stilts. There's a wooden bench in the hallway and I plop down on that. This day couldn't possibly get worse, could it? I can hear Mrs. DiCastillo speaking loudly into the phone in her office, though I can't make out the words she's saying.

The secretaries in the main office are talking about their plans for the weekend, until a ringing phone interrupts their conversation. A few kids pass by in the hall, sneaking glances and whispering behind their hands. There might as well be a big, flashing neon sign over my head that says: "*IN TROUBLE WITH THE PRINCIPAL!*" I want to crawl under the bench and die.

Then I spot the rabbit.

He comes lolloping out of the library like he hasn't a care in the world, freezes when footsteps sound in the hallway, and then scurries under a rack of large paper rolls. He crouches there, nibbling a piece of red paper that's hanging low to the floor, until two kids walk past and the coast is clear again. He pokes his nose out, wiggles it, and looks like he's about to carry on his way again down the hall to the primary wing.

"Tiny," I call in a loud whisper. "Here, Tiny! Come here!"

The rabbit stops and his ears swivel towards me.

"You want a banana?" Not that I have a banana, but he doesn't know that.

He turns his head and looks at me. Then he sniffs the floor in front of him and takes a few hops down the hallway.

"Not that way!"

He stops and looks at me again, his nose wiggling. Then he hops a little further down the hallway.

I groan. Trying to be as quiet and unnoticeable as possible, I get to my feet and follow after him. As he makes his way down the hallway, he keeps hopping and stopping. Hopping and stopping. At last, I'm almost close enough to grab him.

I try my best Libby voice: "Come here, little bunny. I promise I'll always be extra-super nice to you if you just let me pick you up. I'll get you carrots. And bananas. And Cheerios."

I'm so close. I just need to reach out and scoop him

up. He pauses, as if to consider my offer.

I'm slowly, ever so slowly, reaching my hand out towards him, when a door opens behind us. The rabbit's ears go bolt upright, he thumps the floor with his back leg, then takes off running full speed down the hall, his feet slipping and sliding under him on the slick linoleum floor.

"Drew Montgomery!" Mrs. DiCastillo shrills, tripping towards me on her high heels. "Where do you think you're going?"

"I—I wasn't going—"

"Do you have *any* idea how much trouble you're in, young man?" She sets her hands on her hips. "Honestly! Your behaviour is just beyond belief! I recommend you return to my office and stay there until you're told otherwise!"

I trudge back down the hall and into her office. She follows behind me, her gaze like laser beams on my back.

I plunk down on the chair.

"Your mother will be here in a few minutes," she says. "I have other business to attend to. You will stay here until your mother arrives. Do not move!" And she leaves the office, closing the door firmly behind her.

Mom? Oh no!

The next ten minutes crawl by slowly. I sit watching the clock, beginning to wonder if it's stopped, or maybe the hands are actually moving backward. Then I hear my mother's voice in the hallway. If my stomach felt like it had dropped onto the floor, now it plunges into the basement.

The principal directs Mom into her office and into a chair. The look Mom gives me could peel the paint off walls.

Mrs. DiCastillo sits at her desk and laces her fingers together. "Well, I am sorry to have to call you in from work over this, Mrs. Montgomery. But as you know, our school has a strict policy regarding any form of bullying. I'm afraid we're going to have to give Drew a three-day suspension."

A suspension? Me? I thought only really bad kids got suspensions. I remember hearing last year about a kid in grade six getting suspended for kicking a teacher. There's no way I've done anything anywhere near *that* bad.

Mom sighs heavily.

"Drew, go get your things," Mrs. DiCastillo says. "Your mom will take you home now."

I slink out of the office to go get my gym bag and backpack.

A thump from the primary wing draws my attention and there, again, is the rabbit, crouched nervously on the floor. His ears are pointed right at me.

"Tiny!" I whisper.

I'm debating whether to risk trying to catch him again or do as I've been told, when a bunch of grade two girls comes spilling out of the grade two classroom squealing with delight.

"A bunny!" one girl cries.

"Where did you come from?" says another.

And then Libby's voice rings out over all the others, "Tiny! How did you get to school?"

Oh no!

Libby scoops Tiny up and nuzzles him. I can't tell for sure from this distance, but it looks like he nuzzles her right back. Unbelievable!

Then Ms. Lee, their teacher, comes out of the class-room. "What's this? A bunny? Where did he come from?"

Libby pipes up. "This is Tiny. He's my bunny! Well, mine and my brother's."

All the other girls have crowded around Tiny and are oohing and aahing over him. Libby is positively beaming.

"And how did he get here?" Ms. Lee asks.

"I don't know," Libby says. "He was just here in the hallway. I guess maybe Drew brought him."

"Did he have permission?"

"I . . . I guess so." Libby shrugs.

"Who is Drew's teacher, Libby?" Ms. Lee says.

"Mr. Plonski."

"Well, we'd better talk to Mr. Plonski. Girls, back into class. Libby, come with me." Ms. Lee leads Libby down the hall towards me.

I want to turn and run, but I'm like a deer caught in the headlights. All I can do is stand there and watch them getting closer and closer.

Then the door to the principal's office opens behind me and Mom and Mrs. DiCastillo come out into the hall, talking.

Libby spots Mom and her eyes get big and she turns really pale. She tries to hide behind Ms. Lee.

"Oh, Mrs. Montgomery!" Ms. Lee says. "Well, isn't this convenient? Perhaps you can solve this mystery for us."

Mom looks like the last thing she wants to do is solve a mystery. She looks like she'd much rather go home and go to bed.

"Yes?" she says, her voice sounding strained.

"Well, Libby and I—" Ms. Lee glances behind her for Libby. "Libby?"

But Libby's gone.

21
Libby!

Where on earth . . . ?" Ms. Lee says, glancing
around the hallway.

"Libby?" Mom says. "Libby?!"

Then I catch a glimpse of movement slipping
around the corner to the intermediate wing. I think
Mom might have seen it, too. So I point at the front
doors and say, "There she goes!"

All three women dash to the front doors and I take
off running down the hallway in the opposite direction.

Behind me I can hear Mom's confused voice saying,
"Drew? Drew! Oh, I'm so sorry . . . I don't know what's
. . . Drew!" And she comes running after me, clip-clop-
ping as fast as she can in her high heels. "Stop, Drew!"

Just then, the lunch bell rings. And the classroom
doors open and kids begin spilling out into the hallway.

I can hear Mom muttering and apologizing as the sea of kids swamps her. I don't stop. I duck out the side door. Libby is halfway across the playing field now—the rabbit still clutched firmly in her arms. I can see his ears bouncing up and down with each step she takes.

"Libby!" I call, but that only makes her little legs move faster.

I race after her.

She runs through the gate and into the parking lot, heading for the golf course next to our school. I force myself to run faster.

Libby stumbles as she runs onto the golf course green, almost dropping the rabbit, but she rights herself and runs on.

I'm catching up with her. She's only a few feet ahead of me now. "Just stop! Please stop!"

Then, down the fairway, I hear someone cry, "FORE!"

Oh no!

"Libby, get down!" I yell.

A golf ball comes whizzing towards us. I duck and stumble, as the ball thuds to the ground just a few feet ahead of me. It bounces over my head, missing me by bare inches.

"Geez!" I say through clenched teeth.

Libby trips again and this time she goes down—somehow still hanging onto the rabbit. She tries to get up and run again but I'm by her side, grabbing her arm. "Stop! What are you doing? Are you trying to get us killed?"

"I'm—I'm running away!" She gulps. Tears are sliding down her cheeks.

"What? Why?"

"Because they'll take Tiny away. They can't take Tiny away!"

Down the fairway, I hear another voice shout, "FORE!"

"Could we at least get off the golf course? Please?"

Libby is crying too hard to talk, but she allows me to lead her off to the side of the fairway just as another golf ball thuds onto the grass. We sit under a tree. The rabbit's eyes are bugging out of his head.

"I think you're squishing Tiny," I say.

Libby looks down and laughs and sobs at the same time. She sets Tiny on her lap and starts stroking him. He flattens himself out and relaxes.

"We'll figure something out, Libby," I say, trying to sound reassuring. I know Mom and Dad are going to make her give up the rabbit, but I can't stand to see her crying like this. "We'll find a way to keep Tiny."

"Promise?" Libby sniffles.

"I promise." And I really mean it.

"Drew! Libby!" Mom comes panting up to us. "What is with the pair of you? Are you trying to—?" Then she spots the rabbit. "Good lord! That's—that's a real rabbit!"

"Yes, yes, it is," I say.

"I thought it—it looks just like Tiny Junior!"

"Mom," I say. "This is Tiny Senior."

Mom's mouth drops open.

Libby starts crying all over again.

🥕   🥕   🥕

Mom herds us back to the school where Mrs. DiCastillo and Ms. Lee are waiting, looking both irritated and concerned at the same time. After another meeting with Mom in the principal's office, they decide Libby should be excused from school early today too. We take the rabbit and climb into Mom's car.

"I don't know what to think," Mom says. "I'm completely shocked and disappointed. With both of you."

Nobody says a word on the drive home. Libby is snivelling on and off in the back seat, hugging Tiny to her. Tiny, being a rabbit, doesn't make any noise. Mom stares straight ahead, clenching and unclenching the steering wheel. And I stare out the passenger window at the passing houses and streets, trying to make myself invisible.

"I just can't understand it, Drew." Mom says at last. "What on earth would possess you to do such a thing?"

At first I'm not too sure which "thing" she's referring to—running off after Libby or dumping tuna on Maya and Ally's clothes. I decide to stick with a safe answer. "I dunno."

"You don't know? You don't know why you'd bring a can of tuna to school and pour its contents on two girls' clothes?"

Oh. That thing.

"I was defending myself."

"Defending—? Drew! What they wrote on the whiteboard is nothing in comparison to what you did!"

I stare at the floor. "They didn't write on the board, Mom."

The car swerves. "What?"

"No, that was Toby Neville."

The car lurches. "And what did you do to Toby Neville?"

"Nothing! I didn't do anything to him!"

"So you terrorized those girls for nothing?"

"*No!* They deserved it! They've been horrible to me all week. And then they ambushed me at the library. Me and Tabitha! And they sprayed us pink! You have no idea how embarrassing that is!"

Mom just stares at me, until she has to pay attention to the road again or risk being hit by a big garbage truck coming in the opposite direction.

"All I have to say, Drew, is if you felt you were being

bullied, why didn't you tell your teacher or come talk to me?"

I stare at my feet. "I dunno."

"It never once entered your mind to talk to someone about it?"

"I guess not."

She sighs heavily. "Your father is not going to be very happy."

I want to sink into a puddle.

A few minutes later, we pull into the driveway behind Dad's SUV. A white truck with a cartoon cockroach on the side and the name *BUGS BE GONE!* is parked beside it.

Uh oh. I'd forgotten about the exterminator.

Just as Mom, Libby, and I climb out of the car, Dad and a man with a *BUGS BE GONE!* cap on his head come walking around the side of the house.

"Can't say as I can find any evidence of rats, Mr. Montgomery," the exterminator says, pushing the cap back on his head and scratching his forehead. "Pretty clear something chewed through the legs of your kid's bed, but I couldn't tell you what that could be. It sure wasn't rats."

"Well, thanks very much for your time," Dad says, and then he shakes the exterminator's hand, and the man gets into his truck and drives away.

"What are you guys doing home so early?" Dad

turns to us, looking both surprised and confused.

Mom sighs. "We'll talk about it inside. Let's just say I think I've found our rats." She gestures to the rabbit in Libby's arms.

This time Dad's mouth drops open.

22
Please! Please! *PLEASE!*

Mom and Dad send Libby and me to our rooms while they have a talk downstairs. I spend the time cleaning out my closet. Libby, I'm sure, spends the time playing with the rabbit in her room.

I make a pile of my clothes in the middle of the floor, then start pulling the rabbit's things out. And believe it or not, I start to feel sad that the rabbit is going to be sent away. True, the furry beast has made my life miserable this last week and all I've wanted to do is get rid of it. But I've kind of got used to his little whiskered face peering through the baby gate at me every time I walk into my room, and the warm lump by my feet when I wake up in the mornings, and the way he twitches all over when he's eating something he really likes.

Finally, Mom and Dad call Libby and me to the

kitchen. I follow her downstairs. She's still carrying Tiny. He gives me a sad look over her shoulder. I wonder if his feet have touched the ground since we left school.

Dad points at the table and we both sit.

Mom sighs. "You kids have a lot of explaining to do. So you better start."

I glance at Libby. She looks like she's about to burst into tears again, so I take a deep breath and start talking. I tell them how we found the rabbit in the box and how Libby convinced me—I leave out the bit about my bike—to hide the rabbit in my closet. I tell them how the rabbit kept me up all night and ate my gym strip and how that started the war with Maya and Ally. I tell them how the rabbit escaped and got into the pantry and how he must've chewed the legs off my bed so Dad had to call the exterminator. And I tell them how I took the rabbit to school so he wouldn't get found, and then how he escaped from my backpack and I was trying to catch him when Libby found him in the hallway.

Mom and Dad just sit there quietly, listening.

"Drew," Dad says when I'm finished, "to say we're disappointed is an understatement."

"We thought we raised you better than this!" Mom says. "All this lying and sneaking around . . ." She raises her hands and then drops them back to her sides, shaking her head.

Then Dad says, "Drew, do you even realize what you did was wrong?"

Mom crosses her arms.

I hang my head.

"I'm afraid you're grounded for the next month. No TV, no computer, no video games, no comic books, no iPod."

Not that I haven't been going without half those things since the rabbit decided they made a good afternoon snack, but it still doesn't feel good to be told you're cut off for the next month.

"And Libby," he says. "You *know* how we feel about pets."

Tears well up in Libby's eyes.

"Mom has allergies."

"Well, actually," Mom admits, "rabbits are one of the few animals I'm not allergic to."

Dad gives Mom a look that says, "You're not helping!"

"Your dad and I work full time," Mom says quickly. "We don't have time for a pet. Who'll feed it and clean up after it?"

"But we will!" Libby says. "We've been taking care of Tiny all week all by ourselves!"

"What if we go on vacation?" Dad says.

I shrug. "Tabitha has rabbits. I'm sure she can take care of him."

"Pets cost money," Mom says. "Who will pay for food and a cage and vet bills?"

"Drew and I can get a paper route! Or we can do yard work! Or babysitting! Or—"

"Vegetables are cheap," I add. "So's newspaper. And dandelions are free."

"You'll get bored of it!"

"I'd never get bored with Tiny!" Libby protests.

Mom sighs.

Dad holds up his hands. "Enough! We simply cannot have a rabbit."

The tears Libby has been holding back overflow and she starts sobbing again.

"Hey, now," Mom says and lifts Libby—rabbit and all—into her arms. "It's not the end of the world."

"Y-y-yes it is! I lo-o-ove Tiny. Y-ou-ou can't take him awa-a-ay!"

Dad sighs. "You'll understand when you're older, Libby." And he goes to the desk in the kitchen and pulls out the phone book.

Libby starts crying louder. Mom carries her out of the room.

"If you're going to call the animal shelter," I say, "they don't have space."

Dad's eyes narrow. "Oh? And how would you know?"

"I, uh, called them yesterday."

"Oh, really." Dad dials the number anyway. "Yes, hello there. My family has a rabbit we'd like to give up for adoption. . . . Oh? Well, how long do you expect it'll be until there is space? . . . That long, eh? . . . Well, can you call me when space becomes available? . . . All right, thanks." Then he gives his name and phone number and hangs up the phone. He gives me a look that says, "Don't say a word." So I don't.

Mom comes back into the kitchen then. She's still carrying Libby, who's still holding Tiny and still crying, but at least she's stopped wailing hysterically.

"What did the animal shelter say?" Mom says.

"They have no space." Dad sighs.

"Oh." Mom considers this for a moment, then she turns to me. "You said you found the rabbit in a box?"

I nod.

"Was there anything written on the box? Maybe a name? Maybe we could track down the original owners that way?"

"Unlikely." Dad shakes his head. "This wouldn't be the first unwanted pet dumped out here. It's unlikely we'll ever find the owner."

Mom sighs.

"Please, can we keep him?" Libby says. "Please! I promise I'll always keep my room clean and eat all my vegetables and go to bed on time! Please! Please! *PLEASE!*"

"Libby," Dad says and then sighs. "Oh, I suppose we can keep him—"

Libby squeals so loud Tiny's eyes almost pop out of his head.

"—but just until we can find him a good home!"

But Libby is cheering so loud, I don't think she even heard him.

At this point, Tiny seems to have decided he's done being held and he starts wiggling and scrabbling to be put down. Mom sets Libby down so she can set Tiny on the floor. The rabbit flips his ears and then starts hopping around the kitchen, sniffing everything.

"Don't let him run away now," Mom says.

"I won't," says Libby, crouching on the floor beside the rabbit.

"Here, I'll get him some vegetables," I say, take two steps towards the fridge and then freeze. I glance at Mom.

Mom's eyebrows are raised. "Well, that's another mystery solved, I suppose. I knew I didn't dream I bought those Brussels sprouts!"

I bury my head in the fridge, so no one sees the guilty grin on my face.

Dad stifles a laugh.

"He is kind of cute, isn't he?" Mom says, watching the rabbit hopping around the kitchen, rubbing his chin on the kitchen cupboards and the stove and the fridge. "Give him some floppy ears and some black spots and he'd look a lot like Natalie's old bunny, Flopsy."

I feed the rabbit some lettuce. He chows down on the leaf like he hasn't eaten in hours. Come to think of it, he hasn't eaten in hours. I get him another leaf and some parsley and a carrot, too.

"Tiny, huh?" Dad says, watching the rabbit nibbling his salad.

"Cuz he's so cute and tiny." Libby beams.

"Hey, what's this?" Mom says, picking up a flyer from the phone desk that says *FOUND: BIKE!* and has a picture of a bike that looks awfully familiar. My stomach jumps back on the roller coaster and plunges through a double loop the loop.

"Oh, that?" Dad says. "I saw that on my way to work. It's probably the only good news we've got all day. Turns out Mr. Harvey down the road was walking his dog up in the woods and found Drew's bike. Guess the thieves dumped it there when they were done joyriding with it."

"Well, that is good news," Mom says. "It's too bad it looks like it's broken."

"Yeah, Mr. Harvey said it's pretty busted up. But nothing that can't be fixed. He's going to drop it off later today."

I'm starting to feel sick.

"Drew, are you okay?" Mom asks. "You look kind of pale."

"I—no—I mean yes! I mean . . ." I hang my head. I want to let them go on believing my bike has been stolen and dumped in the woods. But I just . . . *can't*. "My bike wasn't stolen," I say quietly.

"What?" Mom says.

"Then what happened—?" Dad's confused look turns to a frown. "Drew?"

"It was me," I say. "I went over a jump in the woods . . ."

Dad takes a deep breath.

"Drew!" Mom says. "What did we tell you about going into the woods?"

"And taking jumps?" Dad says.

I hang my head lower. "I know. I know. Believe me, I've learned my lesson. Please don't call the police."

"The police?" Dad says. "Why would we call the police?"

"I . . . uh, won't I have to go to jail for lying to them?"

"What?" Mom laughs. "For heaven's sake, no. But we will have to call them to tell them we found your bike."

"And that it was never stolen," Dad says.

"And they may want to have a few words with you about honesty."

Mom sighs.

Dad sighs.

And then they ground me for another month.

23
In the End

The school bus drops me, Libby, Tabitha, and Quentin at the bus stop at the top of our road. As we climb off, the bus driver says, "Have a good summer. See you in September."

As we trudge home, Libby skips ahead.

"So how's it feel to be ungrounded?" Tabitha asks.

"I dunno. I haven't got used to it yet." I laugh.

"I heard Maya's still grounded," Quentin says. He seems to have got used to the idea that Tabitha and I are now friends. And *just* friends. She comes over at least once a week to play with Tiny. And sometimes she brings Lolly and Oscar with her.

I shrug. "As long as her and Ally steer clear of me, I don't care." Somehow—okay, it was Tabitha—Mrs. Di-Castillo learned that Maya and Ally had ambushed us at the library and she called their parents. I heard they got grounded even longer than me. Plus Mrs. DiCastillo's been keeping an eye on them. Now they both go out of their way to avoid me. Which suits me just fine.

In the backyard, we catch up with Libby. She's pulling weeds in her little garden patch. She's got lettuce, parsley, carrots, and radishes growing. When Mom started complaining about needing a second fridge for Tiny's vegetables, Libby decided she needed to plant a garden. Mom kept saying no:

"We don't have time for a garden."

"Who will water it and weed it?"

"Gardens cost money."

She should've known she was fighting a losing battle.

Libby tosses the weeds into the compost box we built by the back fence and the four of us head into the house. We toss our shoes and backpacks and head for the kitchen.

Mom pops her head out of the office door. "There's iced tea and blueberry muffins in the kitchen," she says. She's working from home three days a week for the whole summer. Which means I'm not stuck babysitting Libby every day. I think she's always felt guilty for leaving me and Libby by ourselves all the time, because she's been trying extra hard. Snacks after school. Notes in our lunches. That kind of stuff.

"Tiny! We're home!" Libby calls.

In the living room, Tiny is stretched out on the couch, having a nap. He's not so tiny anymore. He weighs ten pounds now and looks like he might grow even bigger. Tabitha has told me he's a Flemish Giant. He's so big, he takes up over half the couch. Even though he's still not as enormous as the rabbit in the picture from Libby's library book, he's the biggest rabbit I've ever seen. His ears swivel in our direction, and he sits up, yawns and stretches. Then he hops off the couch, his giant ears pointed towards us, and bounces out into the hallway, happy to see his humans again.

Libby gives him a good scratch behind his ears and then he hops after us into the kitchen. I get him some veggies from the fridge and put them into the large ceramic dog bowl with bones all over it. Beside it, two other bowls—one plain white bowl for water and a small bowl labelled "KITTY" for pellets—sit on a plastic mat in the corner of the kitchen. We searched all over for bowls for bunnies, but they don't seem to exist. Tiny gallops over and practically crashes head first into the food. You'd think he hadn't eaten in days, not hours.

At first, Dad wanted to put Tiny in a hutch in the backyard, but Mom and Libby didn't like that idea since old Flopsy had met an unpleasant end in a hutch in the backyard. Libby had brought home her library book again and she and Mom were constantly reading bits of rabbit care information to Dad. Finally, he just threw his hands up and said, "Okay, all right. The rabbit can stay inside!"

Mom and Dad talked about buying a cage, but all the cages at the pet store were just too small. So in the end, Tiny stayed in my closet with the baby gate. And then, when it became clear the baby gate couldn't keep him in, without the baby gate. During the day, Tiny likes to sleep on the couch and he sleeps with me almost every night. And he's finally quit peeing on my bed. I guess he just wanted me to be nice to him. But he still has a taste for electronic cords and cables. And comic books. And gym strip. Fortunately, we've all learned about bunny proofing.

We each grab a muffin and a glass of iced tea and pull up chairs around the kitchen table. Tiny's finished gobbling his lettuce and parsley and comes over to nudge our ankles and beg for nibbles of muffin.

Libby plops a blueberry on the floor and it's gone in seconds. Tiny licks his lips and stands on his hind legs looking for more.

"Libby! He'll get fat!" I say, but have to admit it's hard to say no to that face.

Mom comes into the kitchen then. "Libby, you know human food is bad for him. Give him some more parsley instead." She opens the fridge and Tiny practically falls over himself as he races over to her.

We all laugh.

"Is there anything that rabbit does besides eat?" Quentin says, stuffing half a muffin into his mouth.

"Libby's teaching him rabbit agility." Tabitha winks at Libby.

"Teaching him *what*?" For the first time since I've known him, Quentin almost chokes.

"You know," I say. "Like dog agility. With jumps and stuff."

"Okay, this I have to see." Quentin crams the other half of the muffin into his mouth.

"He's not really good at it," Libby says. "He always wants to go under the jumps instead of over them. Lolly is way better at it."

"Come on, let's go set up the jumps and show Quentin." Tabitha pushes back her chair.

"Don't forget," Mom says, "you've got your papers to do, Drew."

"I won't."

I had to get a paper route to help pay for rabbit supplies. And to help pay for my bike to get fixed. And to get new computer cables for my computer. And some new earbuds for my iPod. But it's not so bad. By the end of the summer I should have it all paid off and then I can start saving for something I really want.

We all follow Libby out to the garage to get the agility stuff. It's really just a bunch of cardboard boxes and tubes the two of them put together and painted. When they've got it set up in the backyard—two jumps, a tunnel, and a "pause box" at the end for Tiny to jump onto to get a treat—they come back inside and get his harness and leash.

Libby finally got to use the pale-blue harness to walk Tiny, but he's since outgrown it. And the bigger red harness Mom got for him last month. And the even bigger green harness she got for him a couple weeks ago. His latest harness is one made for dogs and, you guessed it, has bones all over it. He doesn't seem to mind, though.

Once he's clipped into his harness, Libby attaches his leash and he hops outside. He loves it in the backyard. Dad jokes we don't need a lawnmower anymore, Tiny does such a good job trimming the grass. Mom got him a big puppy pen and we just move it around the yard every few days. Otherwise he trims the grass so short it looks like a golf green on a golf course.

"All right, Tiny," Libby says. "Let's show Quentin how you jump." She sets the rabbit in front of the first jump. "Okay, jump!" She leans down and taps him on the bum with her hand.

He hops forward and leaps over the three rungs of the jump.

"Okay now, tunnel!"

He stops and eyes up the tunnel, tilting his head so he gets a good look at it. At first he tries to go around it, but Libby heads him off and he scoots through the tunnel. It's a bit of a squeeze, but he pops out the other side.

"I think we may need a bigger tunnel," Tabitha says.

"With Tiny, we need bigger everything," I say.

"Jump!" Libby says, tapping Tiny on the bum again.

This time, he seems to have had enough. He grabs the bottom rung of the jump in his teeth and pulls it out. Then he squeezes under, knocking the other two rungs off the jump. He hops onto the pause box and stands on his hind legs, looking for his treat.

We all laugh.

"Silly rabbit," Libby says, giving Tiny a few rabbit pellets as a reward and stroking his head.

"You should see Lolly," Tabitha says. "She flies over

the jumps so fast it's hard to keep up."

"Crazy," Quentin says. "Never thought rabbits were so smart."

Yeah, me neither. Not until I had one.

Tabitha resets the jumps and she and Libby take Tiny through the course a few more times. After the fourth time, he's totally lost interest and just wants to eat grass. He knocks the last jump flat and hops away so the girls can't catch him. Then he leads them around the yard in a game of chase that he's clearly enjoying more than they are. Eventually, though, with a bit of help from me and Quentin, we catch him again and take him inside, along with his jumps and stuff.

By that time, Dad is home. He and Mom are standing in the kitchen talking.

"Drew? Libby?" Mom calls. "Can we talk to you for a minute?"

Uh oh. I run a quick mental checklist of everything I could be in trouble for. I took out the garbage and recycling yesterday. I haven't had any complaints on my newspaper route. In fact, I got a tip just last week from the old lady on the corner. It must be that C- in social studies. But if it's about my report card, then why would they need to talk to Libby?

I follow my sister into the kitchen.

Dad has his hands on his hips. Mom's arms are crossed. Oh, this can't be good.

"We just got a phone call," Dad says, "from the animal shelter."

Oh.

Libby's eyes get big. "Bu-u-ut you said we could keep Tiny!"

"No, what I said was, we can keep him until the animal shelter has space. And they just called to tell us they have space."

My stomach sinks. I'd really gotten used to having the furry monster around. I tried to picture the house without Tiny. No warm body tucked up against my legs in the morning. No whiskery face begging treats in the kitchen. No bunny fur on the couch. No lawn circles in the backyard. It would never be the same.

"But what about all the stuff we got him?" I say. "And Libby's teaching him agility!"

"We love Tiny!" Libby says, her lower lip trembling.

Mom smiles and wraps Libby in a hug. "I know. So that's why your dad and I have decided we should keep him."

"Really?" I glance at Dad.

He nods, a smile tugging at the corners of his mouth.

"You guys have proved you can take care of him," he says.

"Thanks, Dad," I say and give him a hug.

He hugs me back. "Hey, I was thinking, how about we go bike riding this weekend?"

"Promise?"

He leans down and looks me square in the eye. "Promise. Besides, now we have a lawnmower that's never gonna need repairs."

I grin at him.

"Tiny! Tiny!" Libby goes running into the living room. "We get to keep Tiny!"

She comes back, toting the rabbit with her. He's so big now, she can barely carry him on her own. "Um, Drew," she says. "You should check your backpack."

"What's wrong with my backpack?" I run into the hallway. My backpack—my new backpack—is sitting in the middle of the floor, a giant hole chewed in the side, and my gym strip—my *new* gym strip—is lying beside it. Actually, more like *pieces* of my gym strip. I sigh. Then I groan. Then I laugh.

In the end, I'd have to say having a rabbit is definitely less boring than a pet rock.

Acknowledgements

Thanks to my family and friends for your love, support, and encouragement. Without you, I'd never have dared to follow my dreams. Thanks also to those who've contributed to making this book a reality, particularly Linda Au Parker and Deanna Dionne. Also thanks to the members at RabbitsOnline for the invaluable rabbit care information as well as the encouragement and comradery of all the fellow bunny slaves there. And thanks to all the writers over the years—everyone at Backspace, the SCWBI Blueboards, the KBoards, Crit-Club, the In the Middle Critters, and the various other private groups I've been a part of—for helping me improve my craft, offering guidance, and even giving me the occasional butt-kicking when I needed it.

About the Author

Rachel Elizabeth Cole writes a mix of genres, from heartfelt to humorous, but her favourite will always be middle grade fiction. When she's not writing, Rachel works as a graphic designer specializing in book covers. Her favourite season is autumn, she prefers tea to coffee, and wishes every morning began at ten a.m. Even though she hates the rain, Rachel lives just outside Vancouver, British Columbia, with her husband, their two sons, and two very spoiled house rabbits.

Find out more at *www.rachelelizabethcole.com*